LIFT ME TO THE SKY AT SUNRISE

LIFT ME TO THE SKY AT SUNRISE

MARTIN PETERSON

Northwest Publishing, Inc.
Salt Lake City, Utah

Lift Me to the Sky at Sunrise

All rights reserved.
Copyright © 1995 Northwest Publishing, Inc.

Reproduction in any manner, in whole or in part,
in English or in other languages, or otherwise
without written permission of the publisher is prohibited.

This is a work of fiction.
All characters and events portrayed in this book are fictional,
and any resemblance to real people or incidents is purely coincidental.

For information address: Northwest Publishing, Inc.
6906 South 300 West, Salt Lake City, Utah 84047

JAC 7.19.94

Edited by: R. Larsen

PRINTING HISTORY
First Printing 1995

ISBN: 1-56901-332-2

NPI books are published by Northwest Publishing, Incorporated,
6906 South 300 West, Salt Lake City, Utah 84047.
The name "NPI" and the "NPI" logo are trademarks belonging to
Northwest Publishing, Incorporated.

PRINTED IN THE UNITED STATES OF AMERICA.
10 9 8 7 6 5 4 3 2 1

To my father, Orville Peterson,
for teaching me a great love of the Western novel.

ONE

The old man stirred under the buffalo robes. Medicine Elk rolled onto his side and opened his eyes. The teepee was empty in the soft dawn light. There was no flame left in the fire, just smoke rising in wisps from the embers.

He huddled deeper into the warm buffalo robes. He knew that there was no more firewood to stoke the fire against the freezing February chill. He was too frail to cut and gather his own firewood anymore from the nearby cottonwood trees that lined the Big Horn River Valley. If he wanted firewood now, he had to ask his relatives and friends. They never refused him, but it humbled the proud warrior.

His stomach gnawed at him as he huddled in the buffalo robes. It had been three days since he ate his last piece of dried buffalo jerky. Food had been scarce this winter. The snows had come in late October, early for the season, and never let up. The summer and fall were too short so the tribe had not been able to lay in enough jerky and pemmican. Now, in February, the food was already being rationed.

They depended on the few deer and rabbits that the braves had been able to down with their arrows in the surrounding river valley. The area was hunted out, though, and the braves were often gone for two or three days. When they returned, they always split up the carcasses among the families. Medicine Elk tried to be close when the hunters came back, but often he didn't get more than a small hunk of fresh meat. If he had a woman, she would be there to fight for his portion.

On these winter mornings, the Crow camp did not rouse very early. There was no reason to get up at dawn. The cold frost enveloped the valley and the Indian teepees, creeping into every crevice and hole. It froze the meat and water skins, and caused the fires to sputter in frustration as they tried to overcome the frigid air. It was two hours after sunrise, but only a few courageous ones had ventured from their teepees. If the afternoon was warmer, then they would go out to cook a meal and visit with their friends.

Medicine Elk poked his aging head out from under the buffalo robes. He was alone, as always. His wife had been dead for six winters now. She had given him three sons, but they were gone now. Two of them died in a battle with the Blackfoot when they were still young men. Even though they died the proud death of a Crow warrior, he mourned them. He had cut off part of a finger for each of them. It was Crow tradition.

The youngest son was killed three summers ago by a white man who trapped beaver in the high places. The white man had ambushed his son, shot him in the back, and left him for the coyotes and magpies. Medicine Elk had cut off part of a third finger the day they found his son's bear-strewn bones.

That son's wife had remarried now and he seldom saw her, even though she lived in the same camp. His granddaughter sometimes came to see him and bring him extra meat or firewood. When it was cold, her mother kept her inside. Medicine Elk missed her visits.

His only daughter had married a fine Crow warrior, but they lived with another band of Crow many days to the south of him. They had five children, two of whom Medicine Elk had never seen. It had been almost four years since he had seen them to the east on the River That Flows Sand. A small hunting party from their band had stopped to trade horses with his party of the Crow tribe. He had seen three of his grandchildren then. Last summer, an old friend from the other band told him of his two new grandchildren.

The loneliness was like a stone in his heart. It never left him and it never let up. He could not go on. As he lay there under the buffalo robes, he knew that the time had come. For years, he had dreaded this time in his life. He always knew that it was inevitable, but he was saddened now because it was so close. Now, he could not put it off any longer.

Medicine Elk tossed back the buffalo robes and struggled to his feet. His joints were inflamed and sore. They snapped as he moved. He could barely hold a knife anymore, even to cut his own food. Creaking, he stood up. It was time to leave.

He looked around the teepee. After a lifetime on the prairies, there wasn't much to take. There was no food, so he didn't need the buckskin shoulder sack. The buffalo robes were too heavy to carry. He wouldn't need the bow and half-dozen arrows. The feathered lance might be useful, but it was too heavy and awkward. He was too old to even drag it very far. He had to take something, though, so he picked up an old stone knife from alongside the smoldering fire.

He had a steel-bladed knife that came from the trading post on the Yellowstone River, but he would leave that. He chose, instead, the black obsidian knife that had been given to him by his grandfather many years before the first white man crossed into Crow land. The crystalline blade had not been chipped in years. It was sharp in only a few places, but Medicine Elk decided to take it anyway. Today, he was more interested in tradition than in defense. He stuck the stone knife unsheathed in his rawhide belt.

He pulled a red and black trading post blanket tightly around his shoulders and stepped through the tent flap. The winter morning slapped his grizzled face. His lungs filled with the Arctic air and he felt his chest tighten. His breath froze instantly into a mist that billowed around his head. Within seconds, his breath formed a hoarfrost on the edges of the blanket. He knew that his mission would not take long today. By noon, it would be over.

There was little activity in the camp. A couple of old women shuffled around in the cottonwoods on the other side of camp. Gathering kindling, he supposed. Medicine Elk ducked to the left behind his teepee. He didn't want anyone to see him. They might try to stop him.

The old man slogged upriver through the snow, south toward the high country. He did not intend to make it to the foothills, but somehow it seemed that he must move uphill. A wounded animal always climbs, his grandfather had told him. Accordingly, a dying man must also climb, he reasoned.

He moved as quickly as he could through the knee-deep snow toward the deepening trees. In the trees, the snow was soft and powdery. Where the sun had touched it, though, a hard crust formed. As Medicine Elk stepped on it, the crust broke through. It exhausted him in less than two hundred yards.

He was in the trees now, at least. The others in camp could not see him anymore. He was alone now, even this close to camp. He sat on a downed tree to rest for a few minutes. His chest hurt from the icy air that froze his lungs and his frail legs ached. The snow had leaked into the holes in his moccasins. There had been no one to sew them this summer. Soon, his feet would be numb.

Medicine Elk gathered himself together, struggled to his feet, and set out again. He faced the sun as it hovered low on the southern horizon. Even at its zenith today, it would not provide much warmth to the High Plains. Nothing would thaw for weeks yet.

He stumbled on, sometimes moving easily through the powdery snow and other times falling through the crust with every step. He skirted the trees and started up the long slopes to the foothills. There were no trees here, only long grass buried under the snow. A few clumps of sagebrush poked their aromatic branches out of the whiteness.

For a while, his feet were cold. Then finally, they stopped hurting. He knew that they were frozen—numb and white inside his moccasins.

At last, he stopped in a long low coulee. He looked around. This was a fine place. The sun was nearing its peak for the day and shone brilliantly on the crystal white snow. All around him was white. The grass was dead, deep under the snow. Even the sagebrush was covered, leaving only lumps of white. Everything below the sky was white and pure and perfect.

The brilliant blue sky blinded him. He squinted against the magnifying properties of the sun on the white landscape. It was so bright that he could no longer open his eyes. He could not go on. He shivered uncontrollably and his teeth chattered. He could no longer feel his feet or his fingers.

There was nothing to sit on here on the hillside, so Medicine Elk plopped himself down into the snow. He would wait here. It would be soon.

The sun seemed to warm him. His feet and fingers did not hurt anymore. He let the trade blanket fall from his shoulders and basked in the new heat. He opened his eyes fully. The light was as if he was inside the sun itself. There were no shadows, no breech of the whiteness. All about him was brilliant and warm. Medicine Elk lay back in the friendly snow and closed his eyes. It was a good day to die.

He could see the face of his beautiful wife in the shining whiteness of the sun. He had almost forgotten how pretty she had been when they were joined. Her soft features and alluring voice now beckoned him to her side. His sons were there in the sky with her. Their lances were held high above their painted horses as they raced from horizon to horizon. He saw them all, his father, his mother, his grandparents, the old people who had crossed over before him. They smiled at him, whispering words of comfort.

Suddenly, though, there was another figure in his dream. It was a white man, a young white man, coming toward him. This white man did not come to harm him, but to be his friend. No white man was his friend.

Medicine Elk felt his mind tense. He had seen white men before, even spoken to them. But he would never let one be his friend. They were the enemy of the Crow. They came from the east to cover the land with buildings and cattle and new grasses. They fenced the water holes and the grassy valleys. They were like grasshoppers that scavenged the land and would someday destroy it.

Medicine Elk fought the dream, but it went on without him. He was powerless to change it.

The white man was with him now, sometimes following him, sometimes leading him. It was summer, hot and dry, and Medicine Elk was thirsty. They were on horseback, running in the deep summer grass. There were blue soldiers chasing them. No, it was his enemy, the Blackfoot, that was chasing them. There was a sharp pain in his side.

It was gone. Everything was white. Medicine Elk cried out for his ancestors to take him. "It is over," he shouted. "You must come to get me."

Out of the misty white dream, the young white man came again. He climbed a cottonwood tree and perched in the crook. The large green leaves twittered softly in the morning breezes as the sun peeked over the eastern hills. Medicine Elk felt himself being lifted into the tree. He could see the hands all around him. No faces, just hands. The only face was the white man. Gentle, but with strength. Innocent despite the blood on his hands.

The white man reached down out of the tree and lifted him. Medicine Elk felt the warm wind on his cheeks. He felt his braided hair rustle against his ears. The white man was pulling him up by the front of his buckskin shirt. He pulled harder and grunted.

Medicine Elk opened his eyes. The flaming red eyes of a coyote were inches from his face. The coyote growled as it jerked on the old man's leather shirt, trying to tear it apart. The hot breath on Medicine Elk's throat and cheeks smelled of blood and rotten meat.

With his right hand, Medicine Elk reached into his belt for the black obsidian knife. He drew it clumsily and slammed it full into the coyote's belly. The wild dog howled and snapped at the man's arm, ripping it open. Medicine Elk jerked the knife again into the underside and felt the hot fluids flood his chest. The coyote jumped away from the Indian, crashed through the crusty snow, and fell headlong into the powder. It twitched twice and was still.

Medicine Elk rolled over to see the dead coyote. It was no dream. He looked at his arm. It was torn and bleeding, but Medicine Elk knew it would heal by spring. He rolled over onto his hands and knees, then struggled to his feet.

He held the battered old knife in his right hand. Blood dripped down his arm, over his hand, down the blade and onto the crystal white snow. It had served him well.

Medicine Elk stood up and looked across the barren whiteness of the long low coulee. It was not a good day to die.

TWO

It was slow, endless torture. The unrelenting August sun imprisoned the nine canvas-covered wagons on the high rolling prairies of the Montana Territory. Six men stood beside one of the stalled wagons, heads down and muttering as they surveyed a broken wheel. The axle and hub lay in the dust among the splintered spokes.

"Well, how long is it going to take to fix this one?" spat Thomas Higgins. His dust-reddened eyes burned like hot coals set deep in an ashy gray beard. His barrel-like chest heaved mightily as he clenched and unclenched his fists. His sunburned cheeks were already starting to show the flush of anger.

Eighteen-year-old Jeremy Higgins stepped back. He knew that the wrong answer from the other men would send his father into another wild rage. Every delay this month had made Jeremy more aware of his father's increasingly violent temper. He had seen his father explode in fury at the oxen. He had stood by helplessly as his mother was slapped one evening because the supper was cold. It was wrong to slap a woman, he knew, but he was no match for his father.

It was already late summer and his father was impatient to reach the gold diggings at Bannack. Thomas had to file a claim and build a warm cabin. The family needed shelter before the snow besieged the high Montana mountain valleys. If they didn't get to Bannack soon, they would be spending their first winter in a canvas tent.

The wagon leader, a gangly scout named Travis, did not hurry his answer. He, too, had seen Thomas Higgins's rage. In his years as an army scout during the War Between the States, he had seldom seen such a violent man. Travis knew violence all too well. His body bore the scars of hard fights and gunshots that had left him with a limp. Seeing the fire building in Thomas Higgins's eyes, Travis was not enthusiastic about facing such violence again.

Travis surveyed the infant Territory that was filling quickly with miners and homesteaders, eager for a new start after the War. The War Between the States had ended that April, leaving thousands of families broken and homeless. Instead of trying to rebuild their burned-out farms in war-torn Missouri, Kansas or Kentucky, they yearned to start fresh in a new land. They sold their homes and headed for the promised lands, the Territories of Montana and Oregon. There were gold diggings in Montana and free land in Oregon. Fortunes could be made and lives could be rebuilt. There was hope.

The children and women had retired to the sparse shade of the stationary wagons, thankful for this break, for any respite from the trek. The wagon train's own dust cloud settled on itself and on the sage hills that rose to the Pryor Mountains in the south. Some of the women brushed the dust from their long skirts and combed their hair, but most were too tired. The smaller children cradled themselves in their mother's laps, the fatigue having sapped their desire to play and explore the new country.

The oxen stomped restlessly in their traces. Sweat trickled down their flanks, etching furrows in caked dirt. The teenage boys moved among the horses and oxen, carefully distributing the dwindling supply of water. They would ration the water for a few more days until they crossed the Big Horn River.

Across the dry prairie expanse, Travis finally spotted a distant spot of green contrasting against the dull browns and yellows. That would be a clump of cottonwoods in a coulee a couple miles north.

"Let's say the day after tomorrow," Travis offered.

"Two days to fix a few spokes?" Thomas Higgins bellowed, his round face flushing red under the gray beard. "What the devil is going to take so long this time, Travis?"

Travis kicked at an anthill with his knee-high Shoshoni moccasins and grunted, "Well, Higgins, by the time we ride down to those cottonwoods and cut us some straight limbs, it'll be dark. We'll start rebuilding the wheel in the morning, but we won't be ready to pull out until after lunch. We'd barely have time to break camp and set it up again."

"We're all pretty tired, Papa," Jeremy added. "The oxen could use some rest, too."

Thomas Higgins roared around and whipped Jeremy savagely with the back of his callused hand. The surprise and force of the blow sent Jeremy sprawling in the dirt.

"You keep your fat mouth out of this, boy."

None of the other men moved. They didn't like Thomas Higgins, but they would not interfere in a family matter. Or rather, none of them wanted to tangle with Higgins.

Stunned, Jeremy gathered his feet beneath himself and stood up. He gingerly touched his lip with the back of his hand and found a smear of blood. He licked the corner of his mouth and tasted the saltiness.

Higgins turned to Travis. "Where are the extra limbs that we have been hauling for these repairs? Doesn't Ben have more tied to his wagon?"

"Nope," Travis answered. "We used the last of 'em three days ago to replace those two cracked spokes on the Randall wagon. And you know good and well that we ain't seen a tree since then that was big enough to cut a spoke from."

"Then we'll leave the wagon here and keep movin'," Higgins demanded.

"No!" yelled the man named Killen as he stepped stiffly toward Higgins. Killen was a small man with a shock of unkempt hair, but every man knew that he was as fast and vicious as a wounded bobcat. No one crossed Killen.

"We're not leavin' nothin' of mine out here."

Higgins tried to placate the wild-eyed man, "Don't worry, Killen. We'll split up your stuff in the other wagons. Your woman can walk. Mine does."

"You can burn in Hades, Higgins. Everybody's full already and we ain't leavin' my belongin's beside the trail to rot."

"Hold it, you two," Travis interrupted as he stepped between them. "We travel together, and we don't leave nobody's wagon unless it can't be fixed at all. That's the way I run my wagon train. Any questions?"

Higgins's eyes narrowed as he surveyed Travis's trail-worn face.

"If you was doin' your job proper, we'd have those extra spokes and we could be rollin' tomorrow. Far as I'm concerned, you're a poor excuse for a wagon leader."

Travis stepped forward and stood full against Higgins.

"When we get to Fort Stillwater, I'm gonna make you eat those words. Nothing would please me more than to kick the livin' devil out of you right now. But we don't need no fightin' amongst ourselves out here. We still gotta spend too many days together."

Higgins shook his head slowly and glared at Travis. "That's where you're wrong."

With that, Higgins wheeled around and stomped back toward his own wagon, kicking up a flurry of dust. Jeremy followed closely, touching his bruised lip with the back of his hand.

He doubted that Mama would ask about it. There wasn't

a need to say much. Maggie knew what was happening to her husband. She could read the meaning of Thomas's harsh words and raging outbursts. He had wanted to leave Missouri alone for the Montana goldfields, but Maggie flatly refused to let the family be separated. Now she staunchly trudged beside the wagon, knowing that her future depended upon her not being a burden to her husband.

The burden was Jennie, however. At fifteen, she wasn't strong enough for months of traversing this nameless land. Mama and Jeremy figured Jennie to be too fragile, and they both often asked if Jennie could ride in the wagon. It seldom happened. Thomas would yell that the oxen had all they could pull as it was. As long as Jennie could walk, she would.

Mama would comfort the young girl at night while Jeremy did most of her chores. If Jennie protested, Jeremy would let her do a couple of the easiest chores. Even with the heat, the cruel pace, poor food and endless days, Jeremy had never heard Jennie complain. She lacked her mother's physical stamina, but at least she had her mother's mental toughness. Jennie would walk until she finally fell from total exhaustion.

"Friendly as a sow grizzly," Travis mumbled as Higgins retreated. "I hope his woman can handle him."

The other three men agreed with low grunts.

When Higgins was gone, Travis addressed the remaining men. "Ben and Powell, you saddle up your horses. We'll ride down to those cottonwoods while the others set up camp. Killen, you make sure it's a good camp 'cause we'll be here an extra day. You two fellas keep your eyes open. We don't need the Crow or Blackfoot surprising us. I've seen 'em out there watchin' us and we don't need them Injuns right now."

He spat in the dirt.

Ben, Powell, Killen and Travis split up and headed for their duties. Killen directed the wagons into a tight circle around his own crippled wagon. He coordinated the efforts of the men and boys in unhitching and posting the oxen. Every axle and wheel was checked for cracks and wear. Each man reapplied grease to the hubs on his own wagon. Before dark, every spoke, axle, and hitch would be checked. Killen helped one of the older men examine and repair the harnesses and tack.

Powell and Ben saddled their horses and grabbed the rifles. Both men rechecked his possibles bag for enough powder, pads and balls for a good fight. They didn't have to tell each other that even three well-armed men were a temptation to roving Indians. The open rolling grass held little cover in case of a fight.

Powell and Ben joined Travis and nudged their horses toward the cottonwoods in the distance. They had ridden only a hundred yards when Travis glanced over his shoulder to see the Higgins wagon pulling away from the others. Travis wheeled his horse around and spurred it into pursuit of the rumbling wagon.

Travis quickly caught the wagon and grabbed the harness of the lead ox. He jerked it back hard. The ox released a wild frightened bellow.

"You let go of that harness, Travis," Higgins yelled, laying the whip to Travis.

"Where the devil are you going?" Travis countered. "Who said you could pack up and leave my wagon train?"

"I don't need the permission of some lame half-blind scout to drive my own wagon anywhere I want to. Now get outta my way."

Higgins viciously laid the whip to the oxen's sweating flanks. Travis hung savagely to the harness as the oxen lunged against the harnesses. His horse bucked and nearly threw him in the midst of the crazed oxen.

Desperately, Travis drew the long-barreled Army Colt from his lap holster and waved it at Higgins. Jennie screamed. Maggie grabbed her and flung her in the dirt behind a large sagebrush.

"Drop that whip, you stupid fool," Travis yelled, brandishing the pistol, "or I'll hang your hide on a sagebrush and let the wind blow through the bullet holes."

Higgins jerked back and sat down heavily on the wagon

bench. His whitened knuckles clenched the whip upright and motionless. Travis released the harness and Jeremy ran up to calm the animals.

"You turn this wagon around and get back with the rest of 'em," Travis ordered.

He held the pistol up in full view, but didn't point it directly at Higgins.

"No one leaves my wagon train unless I decide they're gonna leave."

"Then you better decide that I'm gonna leave," Higgins fired back. "I've been with this train ever since it left Missouri and I'm tired of waiting for some poor fool to fix his broken-down wagon. If they'd take proper care of their wagons, they wouldn't be breaking down and we wouldn't be wasting so much time. We could be at the diggins by now and building our cabins instead of wet-nursing these losers."

"This is hard country, Higgins. You can't expect everybody's luck to be as good as yours. You just ain't hit a good badger hole or a big rock yet, but you will."

Higgins shook his head.

"I'm tired of this hard country of yours and I'm gonna get outta here as fast as I can."

Travis heaved a weary sigh.

"I'm tired of it too, but you don't have a chance of getting across it alone."

"You're bluffing, Travis."

"This is the home of the Crow. Besides the Crow, the Blackfoot and the Sioux use it for their hunting grounds. The only way to travel through Injun country is with enough wagons and guns to make 'em keep their distance."

"You're lyin' to me, Travis. Tryin' to scare me. We ain't seen an Indian in two weeks."

Travis continued, "You might not a' seen many Injuns in the Dakota Territory, but I guarantee that they're here in Montana. I've seen their tracks and smelled their smoke. And it's a sure bet they've seen us."

"I don't buy it."

"You're a fool, Higgins."

"How far to Fort Stillwater?"

Travis leaned across his saddle and shook his head. Frustrated, he replaced his pistol in his lap holster.

In a low voice, he said, "If your wagon holds together, seven days. If not, maybe ten days to two weeks. Without us, you might gain four or five days."

"I'll risk it. How do I get there?"

Jennie and Maggie cautiously rose from their sagebrush refuge and approached the wagon. Jeremy was holding firmly to the lead ox's harness, calming it with soft words and a gentle hand.

Travis shook his head.

"You follow this trail west 'til you hit the Big Horn River. Turn north 'til you hit a bigger river, the Yellowstone. Cross the Big Horn about a mile upstream from the mouth. Stay on the south bank 'til you see a deep canyon to the south. Cross the Yellowstone there and angle north. Fort Stillwater is twelve miles west of the ford. Once you get to the fort, there's a good trail all the way to Bannack."

Maggie hurried to the wagon and reached up to touch her husband's knee.

"Are you sure we should leave the others, Thomas? If it's as dangerous as Travis says, we could spare the four days."

"No," he said tersely. "We're moving out now. I'm tired of waiting."

Higgins cracked the whip above the ears of the lead ox.

"Move aside, boy. Hi-yah, gid-dap there."

Maggie looked up to Travis as the wagon pulled away.

"Is it really that dangerous, Travis?" she asked.

Travis took a deep breath, "You can't go that far in Crow territory without some sort of fight, ma'am. They'll find you. I guarantee it."

From a few yards ahead, Higgins leaned over the side of the rolling wagon.

"You comin', woman?"

She hesitated for a moment and looked up again at Travis.

She searched his grizzled face for some final bit of wisdom or hope. Then with a whirl, she lifted her long skirt and ran to catch her husband. Jennie and Jeremy followed. Travis held his horse tightly as it stepped to follow them.

"I'll bury you, Higgins." Travis yelled at the retreating wagon. "You remember that."

The lone wagon rumbled through the sagebrush as Travis turned back to the others. Ben and Powell sat quietly on the horizon, waiting for Travis. They would have to hurry now to get enough spokes chopped before dark.

The Higgins wagon disappeared in a gray cloud that settled slowly on the aromatic sagebrush.

THREE

By the next afternoon, Jeremy was bored.

At least when they had been traveling with the other wagons, there were thirty other interesting people to chat with during the unending days of walking.

He especially liked to walk with Travis, who told him fascinating tales about Indian customs and military forts. Travis knew the history of the Bozeman Trail and all the Indian tribes. He knew every plant and how the Indians used it for food or medicine. He knew the habits of every animal on the plains. In his thirty-odd years in the West, he had been a soldier, army scout, trapper, fur trader, buffalo hunter and now, wagon master. He had seen most of the United States, but he loved these Western territories. Years ago, he had decided he would do whatever he could to stay here.

One of the strangest tales that Travis told him was how the Plains Indians honored their dead. According to Travis, the closest relatives of a deceased warrior would often cut off a part of one of their fingers as an offering. It was a permanent reminder of the passing of one of their family.

A wife would usually cut off one finger joint as a memorial for her husband, but the husbands would only rarely do it for a deceased wife. A father might do it for his eldest son if he died in battle, but never for a daughter. A mother would often do it for her oldest or favorite son. It was rare, but not unheard of, for a brother to disfigure himself in memory of his closest brother. The self-mutilation would become a permanent memorial that the person had for the deceased. It was a primitive and grotesque custom, but it was the way of the Plains.

Jeremy could not understand why someone would mutilate themselves to honor another person, but he took Travis's word for it. Someday when he got to see Indians up close, he was going to look for a short finger.

Travis had given them all words of warning about the Indian burial grounds. They weren't burial grounds exactly, but rather, usually a platform on four poles or sometimes lashed up in a tree. A white man caught trespassing a burial ground would be immediately and quickly killed. To the Plains Indians, it was a desecration for a white man to tread on the ground near their ancestors.

Once, one of the men had asked Travis about taking a few *souvenirs* from the dead warriors. Jeremy remembered how Travis had glared at him.

"Would you like the Indians to dig up your dead parents and take their gold watches and rings?"

No one ever asked him again. The answer was too simple. Touching a dead Indian warrior or crossing the burial grounds meant instant death if you were caught. For Jeremy, it was an easy lesson to understand.

Killen and Ben were Confederate veterans. They told glowing and gory tales of the battles they had won and lost. Jeremy had heard Ben crying in the night more than once because of the three brothers and two sons he had lost in the fighting. All he wanted now was to start over.

Best of all, Powell had a daughter named Christina. Jeremy had taken a shine to her and they walked together for hours along their wagons. They told each other about their families and their plans for the Montana Territory. Jeremy told her about Missouri and Christina told him about Kentucky. With the War and all, there were hundreds of strange and wild stories to spellbind each other for hours.

Those times had faded now. He could talk to his mother, but her only interests were the new cabin, the garden and all that woman stuff. He wanted to talk to her about Papa and what was happening to him, but he didn't dare. Jennie loved the wildlife and flowers but she knew less about them than he did. And Papa just wasn't talking to anyone.

As Jeremy trudged beside the oxen, he constantly scanned the horizon like Travis had taught him. He had spotted buffalo, antelope and deer on the high dry hills. He had seen coyote, badger, big horn sheep and elk on the open prairies or in the rugged ravines.

He had even seen a prairie grizzly last week. According to Travis, they were the most ferocious creatures on the prairie. The white trappers had been slaughtering them for decades to get the fine heavy fur and excellent meat. There weren't many prairie grizzlies left anymore, and Jeremy considered himself lucky to have seen one.

About midafternoon, Jeremy spotted a movement on a hillside about half a mile to the south.

"Papa, over there," he said, pointing quickly.

Higgins tugged firmly on the reins and the wagon creaked to a halt. He stood up in the wagon seat and pulled his floppy hat down to shield his eyes from the sun.

"Injuns," he said with disgust. He squinted. "Looks like a coupla young ones."

The Indians kicked their ponies in the flanks and raced up the hill. Small puffs of gray dust rose as each hoof fractured the soil. They knew that they had been spotted.

Maggie came running up from behind the wagon, pulling Jennie along smartly.

"Are they going to attack?" Maggie asked breathlessly as they reached the safety of the wagon.

"Not a chance, woman," Thomas bellowed bravely. "They're hightailing it for the next territory. They probably figure we're too well armed. Or maybe they just ain't interested in one lone wagon. Besides, all we got are oxen. No horses for 'em. Oxen don't make a prize for Injuns."

"Do you think they're going for help?" Jeremy asked as the family watched the two horsemen disappear silently over a ridge.

"Naw," his father returned confidently. "They'd need a powerful bunch of them to match two good rifles. Their arrows and lances don't stand a chance out here in the open. We're safe as long as we stay in the open."

He sat back down on the wagon seat and looked around at his family.

"Stay close to the wagon from now on, y'hear?"

Those were the first soft words he had spoken in weeks.

Everyone nodded silently. Maggie remembered what Travis had said about the Indians. She thought about the rest of what Travis had said, especially about a fight. It frightened her and she refused to think about Travis's farewell remark about burying her husband.

Maggie watched the ridge quietly. She stepped up behind Jennie and laid her hands gently on her daughter's shoulders. This was an endless and desolate land and she knew that Jennie shared her own fear and loneliness.

"Mama, when will we see Indians up close?"

"With God's grace, maybe never."

"I would like to see an Indian real close someday, Mama. They wear such funny clothes and they get all painted up and they're always riding horses. Travis says they talk funny, too. He talked to me in Crow one time."

"I'm sure that we look funny to them, too, Jennie."

"Will we see some at Fort Stillwater?"

Maggie smiled, "If we don't see any before then. We'll find one there. Now go walk with your brother for a while."

Maggie climbed onto the wagon seat with her husband as he applied the whip smartly to the oxen. The wagon jerked forward. They were moving west again.

"Thomas, I'm worried about traveling alone."

"Ain't nothing to worry about. We'll be fine."

"I thought we would be okay because we hadn't seen any Indians for so long. Those Indians scared me."

"Don't be silly, woman. You saw 'em retreating. They're afraid of us."

"I don't know."

"As long as we keep our rifles in full view and stay alert, they won't bother us."

They rode for a few minutes without speaking. Jeremy and Jennie were walking ahead of the oxen, probably talking about their first sighting of Indians in the Montana Territory. From up on the wagon seat, Maggie realized how much farther she could see. She wondered why Thomas hadn't spotted the Indians before Jeremy.

"Let's go back to the wagon train with Travis and the others," she finally suggested quietly.

"Absolutely not, woman. Those people are so slow that it'll take us four or five extra days to get to Fort Stillwater. We can get to Bannack a week sooner if we don't have that sorry bunch of Yankees tagging along."

"What difference does it make if it takes an extra week or even a month? Are we in such a hurry that we have to risk our lives?"

"The difference is that we'll never get our cabin built before winter sets in. You wanna spend your first winter living in this wagon or in some wooden lean-to thrown up against a rock pile? We gotta get some land cleared for your garden, too. We need that extra time."

Maggie stared across the endless sagebrush for a few moments, then surrendered.

"Whatever you say, Thomas."

Carefully, she pulled up her skirt and jumped down from the lumbering wagon. Submissively, she resumed her place in the shade of the wagon, praying as she walked.

Late on the second morning after they had left the wagon train, Thomas spotted Indians. Jeremy was trudging alongside the wagon watching for antelope and buffalo tracks. Maggie and Jennie were engrossed in discussions about how to decorate their log cabin and what vegetables to plant in the mountain garden.

Only Thomas saw the five warriors, naked except for loincloths and simple feathered headbands. They sat quietly astride their multi-colored pintos. The feathers on their long lances fluttered gracefully in the prairie breeze. Each horseman had a bow and a quiver of arrows slung across his tan shoulders.

Thomas casually lifted his rifle from the scabbard alongside the wagon seat and laid it across his lap. Nervously, he fingered the trigger guard. Although the Indians still kept their distance, they were not trying to hide this time.

Thomas took a long breath as he watched them. He hoped that Maggie and Jeremy would not see this bold display by the nomads. For a moment, he thought that they might attack the lone wagon as it lumbered along the open prairie. They made no movement, however, and Thomas guessed that they were afraid of the white man's long rifles. There were only two rifles—his and Jeremy's—but even they were more than a match for five Indians armed with only bows and lances. The Indians knew the awesome power of the long rifles. They knew there was too much open grass between them and the wagon.

It was a stand-off for now, but Thomas sensed there would be a confrontation soon. He also knew that it would be nearly a week before they reached the Yellowstone River and the protection of the more traveled section of the Bozeman Trail. The lone wagon rumbled west, leaving the five young braves behind.

Higgins decided that afternoon that they would have to be

constantly prepared for the inevitable fight. He cautioned the family from straying too far from the wagon. He realized, too, that they would be most vulnerable at night, so he began watching for campsites that could be defended by only two rifles.

There were still two hours of good daylight when they passed through a long swale that sprouted patches of willow trees in the moist bottom. There was no water, just heavy grass in the shallow valley between the low hills. Higgins could see how the wagon could be pulled up tight against a stand of willows. That would provide some protection for his family.

Higgins finally pointed to a large stand of willows and said, "We'll camp here tonight."

With that, he reined the oxen to the right and headed them toward the willows.

Maggie was so surprised that she stopped in her tracks. After weeks of complaining about the slow progress they were making, her husband had suddenly decided to make camp early. It was as if the gold fever that had gripped her husband and made him push his oxen and family to uncompromising limits had suddenly softened. She wondered briefly about the Indians, but dismissed it because she had only seen two yesterday. And they were riding away. It didn't make sense.

Maggie hiked up her long skirt and hustled alongside the wagon seat.

"Thomas, we've still got sunlight. We can make a few more miles before dark."

"We're camping here, Maggie. The oxen can use the rest. So can we. Besides, we might not find another good campsite before dark."

"We have enough water and we can cut some firewood here. Let's keep moving 'til dark."

"We're staying here, woman," Thomas said bluntly.

"What's so special about this spot, Thomas?"

Higgins thought about it for the moment as the wagon lurched toward the willows. Finally, he looked into the eyes of the woman that had faithfully trailed beside him from Missouri.

"Protection," he said simply.

Maggie dropped back as the wagon slipped into the deepening grass. It was Indians. She knew that he had seen them again. She shuddered.

"Mama, are we stopping already?"

Jennie was beside her, her eyes quizzing softly. Maggie reached out her roughened hand and stroked Jennie's hair.

"The oxen are tired, dear, and Papa wants to rest them for tomorrow. Besides, we can cook a fine dinner tonight."

Jennie smiled.

"I'd like that."

Higgins pulled the wagon up within a few feet of the small grove of willows.

"Thomas, it's too close to the trees. There isn't hardly any room back there."

He just grunted.

"It stays."

Maggie did not press it. Thomas was right.

Jeremy unhitched the oxen and haltered them to graze in the deep grass near the wagon. He wandered a few yards down the ravine to dig a hole in the sandy bottom. He had only dug about a foot when he hit wet dirt. A few inches deeper and muddy water started to fill the hole. He waited for the hole to fill, then used a cup to dip it out into a small barrel for the oxen. They were running low on water and Travis had taught him this simple lesson in finding water.

Jennie's interests lay more in picking the prairie wildflowers than digging for water, though. She wandered down the ravine, gathering cutleaf daisies and sego lilies to make a gold and white bouquet for Mama.

After securing everything for the night, Higgins surveyed the campsite. A small knoll to the south would make a good lookout for tonight. He would take first watch, then Jeremy. From the knoll, he could see the low hills rise above the trees. No one could get to the wagon without being seen. It was a good spot, he reasoned.

He returned to the wagon to find Maggie starting a campfire.

"No fire tonight, Maggie," he ordered.

"What about supper? I was going to mix up hotcakes and fry bacon and corn biscuits."

"Cold camp tonight," he said harshly. He paused. "I'm sorry."

He looked at her softly for only the second time in weeks and she understood. She could see the fear welling up inside him for the first time since the last days of the War. Fire meant smoke and that would pinpoint their camp. Again, she knew he was right.

"Cold biscuits and dried meat?" she asked.

"Yeah. That's fine."

She nodded and put the wood in the back of the wagon. Maybe they could make a fire for coffee and bacon in the morning. At least they would be on the trail again before the smoke was detected.

"Where are the children?" he asked.

"They went to find water for the oxen."

Thomas's eyes grew larger.

"Which way?"

"Down the ravine, over there," Maggie said, pointing. Suddenly, she realized the danger, too.

"God save them," she whispered.

Thomas grabbed his rifle, leaped over the hitch and loped down the ravine. Maggie gathered her skirt and raced behind Thomas. He quickly spotted Jeremy squatting over his water hole, waiting patiently for the water to seep in.

"Where's Jennie?"

"Uh, I don't know, Papa. I think she walked down there."

With his heart in his throat, Thomas raced down the ravine. He found Jennie a hundred yards away, just around a bend. She was hunched over an anthill, watching the red ants scurry about. Mama's bouquet of prairie flowers was clutched loosely in one hand.

"What the devil are you doing, Jennie?" he yelled at her. "I told you to stay close to the wagon."

He grabbed Jennie by the forearm and roughly dragged her back toward the wagon. Halfway up the ravine, they met Maggie.

"Now you stay with your mother. And don't ever go wandering off again like that. This ain't Missouri."

"Don't be so rough on the child, Thomas," Maggie interrupted. "She didn't know better."

"She does now. Everybody stays close to the wagon 'til we get to Fort Stillwater. I don't want nobody tramping around the hills alone."

Jennie hung her head and Maggie laid her arm across her daughter's shoulders.

"Come on, Jennie, help me get supper ready."

After a cold supper of hard corn biscuits and dried beef jerky, Thomas lay down underneath the wagon.

"Wake me up at dark, Maggie. I'm going to stand first watch tonight but I need to get some sleep. Tell Jeremy he'll have to stand watch later. I'll let him sleep 'til two or three in the morning."

Maggie nodded. She understood. There wouldn't be any more questions from her.

She picked bedding places for herself and the children. Instead of sleeping under the wagon as they usually did, however, Maggie spread the bedrolls out in the grass among the willows. The trees offered more protection.

After the children had lain down under the willows, Maggie pulled the family Bible from a battered trunk in the wagon. The Bible had been a present from her grandmother on the day that she and Thomas were married. Its hard brown cover was now travel-worn and dog-eared. The gold filigree on the front and sides was gone and the imprint on the front was nearly illegible. The edges of each page were dull from daily use, especially the Psalms and the Gospel of Luke, her favorites. In the back, Maggie had entered all the family's births and deaths.

"Mama," Jennie said, "I'm afraid of the Indians. That's why Papa is doing all this, isn't it?"

"Hush, child. Your father is a brave man and he is just being careful. You go to sleep now and let the Lord watch over us. His angels are guarding us, aren't they?"

"Yes, Mama."

After a thoughtful pause, Jennie asked, "Mama, will you read to us?"

"Of course, dear."

Softly, Maggie opened to Psalms. She looked at words but it was already too dark to read. She looked at her worn Bible, and recited the words she knew by heart.

The Lord is my shepherd, I shall not want.
He maketh me lie down in green pastures,
He leadeth me beside the still waters.
He restoreth my soul: He leadeth me in the paths of righteousness for His name's sake.
Yea, though I walk through the valley of the shadow of death, I will fear no evil: for Thou art with me; Thy rod and Thy staff they comfort me.
Thou preparest a table before me in the presence of mine enemies: Thou anointest my head with oil; my cup runneth over.
Surely goodness and mercy shall follow me all the days of my life: and I will dwell in the house of the Lord forever.

Maggie closed her Bible. "Good night, Jennie."

"Good night, Mama."

Maggie slipped away from the bedrolls. She picked up Jeremy's rifle and sat by herself near the wagon. The night was quiet except for a gentle rustle of the night breeze. Maggie loosened her hair from under her bonnet. The trail dust and burning sun had taken its toll on her hair and face. The sun was harsh on her and the dust choked her beautiful skin. Once they reached the gold fields, though, she could start being pretty again.

She watched the darkness set in. It was too dark to see

anything but she sensed that there was no one out there. They were alone.

It was long past sundown when she finally shook Thomas to wake him.

"What's wrong?" he said as he grabbed for his rifle.

"Nothing, dear. You wanted me to wake you to stand guard. Everything is quiet."

"Thanks, Maggie," Thomas said, kissing her on the cheek. It was the first time in weeks. "You get some sleep."

"Good night."

He heard her skirt whooshing through the grass as she retreated toward her bedroll near the children.

The night was quiet and dark. Thomas heard an owl swoop softly into the willows behind the wagon, then lift off to the north. There were small noises in the grass—mice, bull snakes and skunks—but nothing stirred except nature. He watched closely for a long time before convincing himself that the Indians were not interested in them.

A couple hours before sunrise, Thomas felt himself nodding off. They had traveled hard for weeks now, and the sleep that he was sacrificing tonight made him drowsy. He fought it for a while, but finally decided to surrender for a couple hours. He stood up, stretched, and walked over to where Jeremy was sleeping.

He shook Jeremy by the shoulder. "Son, wake up. It's your turn to stand guard. It's only a coupla hours 'til sunrise and I gotta sleep."

Jeremy roused slowly, found his rifle and moved to the knoll. He found a spot about fifty yards from the wagon where he could see all around the willows and up the long low horizon.

Jeremy sat down against a small cutbank. A stand of sagebrush on his left shoulder would keep the morning breeze from chilling him. He could hear his father rustling in his bedroll near the wagon, settling in for some precious sleep.

For a while, Jeremy stayed awake in the cool pre-dawn air, listening to the same sounds of nature that his father had heard all night. The wind rustled slightly, a shadowy coyote moved across a nearby hillside and mice roamed in the grass. The sounds were familiar from the two months on the trail.

Lulled by the quiet and solitude in this desolate world, Jeremy closed his eyes for a moment. He was exhausted, too, drained by the 800-mile walk from Missouri. For just a moment, he would close his eyes, he thought.

He sensed the sunrise just infiltrating the darkness. He was dreaming of kissing Christina, Powell's daughter. It was just a dream, though, because he had never gotten up the nerve to try. Maybe when Christina caught up to them in Bannack, he would have the courage.

In his dream, he heard a soft thump, then another one and another. There was a rustling in the grass near the wagon. Jeremy slowly opened his eyes, expecting to see his father moving about in the soft pre-dawn light.

Suddenly, Jennie screamed. Jeremy was instantly awake, grasping for his rifle. Five warriors were scurrying around the campsite, stabbing the bedrolls viciously with their lances. One wildly painted brave was struggling with young Jennie. He had tied a leather thong around her wrists and thrown her over his shoulder.

Jeremy jerked his rifle to his shoulder but before he could draw up on a target, the invaders had melted into the willows.

Jeremy prayed under his breath and raced toward the wagon at breakneck speed. Why didn't Papa get up and fight? Why was Mama so still? He must still be dreaming, he had to be dreaming.

But Jennie's scream jarred him to reality. He heard horses whinny on the other side of the thicket as the Indians mounted them.

As he leaped over the wagon hitch, he heard the snorting of horses and the slap of quirts on their flanks. The willow thicket that his father had chosen for protection now shielded any shot that Jeremy might have taken. The raiders disappeared into the prairie dawn with their captive.

Jeremy stood over the blood-soaked bedrolls. The grisly

truth slapped him like a thunderbolt that strikes too close. A feathered and painted lance protruded from Papa's bedroll. The morning breeze caressed the delicate feathers, betraying the steel point on the other end. Two long bloody cuts in Mama's bedroll told her story.

The attack had been so swift that neither one had awakened. For a moment he stared at the blood oozing from the slits across their foreheads where the scalps had been sliced hastily. He dropped to his knees beside Mama and stared in disbelief. He touched her face and felt the warm blood on his fingers.

His eyes clouded with tears. It couldn't be true. They couldn't be dead. The tears overflowed freely down his cheeks. His body rocked with spasms of grief and his mind reeled in confusion. He had fallen asleep. He hadn't seen the Indians sneak up on them. He had let them down. And now they were dead. It was all his fault.

His eyes burned as the willows filled with smoke. The wagon was on fire and was already belching huge quantities of acrid smoke. Horrified, he swung around to the wagon, but the tinder-dry wood and canvas were already engulfed in flames. Gone. Too late.

Jeremy dragged the bodies away from the burning wagon and covered them with the blankets of his own bedroll. He stumbled away and collapsed in the tall grass. When the sobs had finally subsided, he looked and tried to shake the grief from his head. He tried to think straight.

Papa and Mama would have to be buried in a decent Christian manner, like he had seen in Missouri. Jennie was gone now, carried off by the Indians.

He walked back to the wagon and watched it billow huge flames. There was nothing left. He moved into the willows where they had all slept. Mama's Bible lay in the grass, kicked open in the scuffle. Its pages twitched softly in the breeze. Mama's canteen was there, so at least he had some water. Papa's rifle was gone, but Jeremy had his own, plus a pouch of balls, gunpowder, and a knife.

Jeremy tried to think again about burying Papa and Mama. He didn't have a shovel to dig the holes—it was in the wagon. He wasn't sure that he could touch their bodies again even if he could dig the graves. Besides, he had to get Jennie back. If he dug the graves, he would never catch up to the kidnappers.

He realized that Travis and the rest of the wagon train would be along later today or tomorrow. They could bury the bodies. Travis's parting comment about burying Papa echoed in Jeremy's mind. He knew that Travis would understand.

FOUR

The trailing was easier than Jeremy expected. The Indian horses left deep prints in the sandy soil as they threaded their way through the grass and sagebrush. He lost them twice where they crossed deep coulees that were chest deep with bulrushes and wild rosebushes. Luckily, Travis had taught him to walk in ever-larger circles to find a set of lost tracks. By doing that, he always found the trail again.

It was hot and still that afternoon, inciting a storm in the west. As the anvil-shaped thunderheads built in the late afternoon, Jeremy prayed that it would not rain. Although it would be cooler, a hard rain would wash away the tracks.

He also knew that the Indians were traveling much faster on horseback than he was on foot. He prayed that he would overtake them before his strength waned.

Jeremy stopped that evening in a deep ravine with a trickle of water and a few scrubby cottonwood trees. The mosquitoes were so thick and hungry, though, that he finally surrendered to an open hillside where the night breezes kept the mosquitoes at bay.

He slept fitfully for only a couple hours that night, worried about Jennie. The rain that sprinkled on him twice during the night woke him up. It never rained hard, though, just enough to dampen Jeremy's clothes. Then it would quit and the wind would kick up. Thankfully, the thunderstorms passed overhead. The trail lay quietly in the night, waiting for him.

At sunrise, Jeremy was on the trail again, walking quickly, running as much as he could. The two-month walk from Missouri had toughened him. His young body could endure an entire day of walking and trotting alongside the wagon without collapsing. He knew he was more prepared for this journey than he had ever been in his life.

Late on the second afternoon, Jeremy topped a ridge that shielded a long, low draw. Suddenly, he spotted three Indians lying on the ground around a dying campfire at the bottom of the draw.

He quickly dropped to his stomach. He loaded his rifle and poised himself for a swift and sure attack.

He watched them lie there, not moving. It was strange, he thought, that they would be sleeping so late in the day. He listened for any sounds, but heard only the wind rushing through the brown drying heads of crested wheat grass. Finally, a magpie swooped down into the campsite. Almost with casual indifference, the magpie strutted over to one of the Indians and started to peck at his face. The Indian was dead.

Jeremy cautiously raised his head above the dry grass and surveyed the hillsides surrounding the draw. The afternoon wind was quieting. There were few sounds, only a meadowlark's lonesome chirruping cry. The Indian horses were gone and the bodies were abandoned.

Jeremy carefully threaded his way through the sagebrush and tall grass. He stayed on his stomach and elbows until he got within twenty yards of the bodies.

Three Indians lay sprawled on the sandy ground. He could see the broken arrow shafts protruding from two of the bodies and a ragged gash on the neck of the third one. A splintered lance was still clenched in his hand. All three were neatly but bloodily scalped.

Jeremy was sure that these were three of the Indians that had attacked his wagon and killed his parents. He had tracked them carefully. He did not understand, though, why were they dead. And where were the others? Most important, where was Jennie?

Jeremy stood up and slowly circled the encampment. He was cautious and careful, scanning the horizon as he surveyed the small battlefield. On three sides, he found scuff marks in the sand where Indians had crawled on their bellies to within a few yards of the Blackfoot. He found Jennie's small bare footprints in the dirt against a low cutbank where she had curled up to sleep.

He finally pieced it all together. These Indians had camped in the ravine the night before, and tied Jennie up near them.

The five Indians had been surprised by another band of Indians, probably another tribe. The intruders had used the cutbank and sagebrush as cover to get close enough to ambush them. There must have been nine or ten attackers, because Jeremy found the hoofprints of a small horse remuda in a draw just over the hill from the massacre. Jeremy also found tracks of two horses riding hard to the north. He figured that two Indians had escaped the attack and were returning to their own people.

Jeremy remembered the tales that Travis had told him about the Indians in the Montana Territory. He recalled Travis's stories about how the Blackfoot hunting parties from the north roamed the Crow territory.

It all made sense now. It had been Blackfoot that had attacked the wagon. Three of them now lay cold and lifeless in the coulee. If Jeremy figured right, Jennie was now a captive of the Crow.

Jeremy followed the new hoofprints to the south at a renewed pace. They were headed toward the Pryor Mountains, a series of dry rugged mountains with little vegetation or wild game. Jeremy followed quickly, easily tracking the dozen or more horses. He knew that one of them carried his sister.

As Jeremy entered the foothills of the Pryors, the land became rougher. Sandstone and shale outcroppings scarred the dry hillsides. Using a fist-sized rock and a sharp aim, he stunned a jackrabbit near an outcropping. He skinned it and cooked it on a small juniper fire under some scrubby pine trees. The branches dispersed the small amount of smoke so that it would not alert the Indians.

After two days of no food, he was weakening. He ate most of the rabbit right off the spit and wrapped the rest in his handkerchief. He could eat it tomorrow as he traveled.

The prairie night was noisy. Coyotes kept up an eerie chorus as the waning half-moon rose brightly over the plains. Rabbits and mice scurried about in the grass and sagebrush, using the darkness as cover for their nocturnal adventures.

Jeremy was alone, though, as he retreated under a sandstone overhang that jutted into a rugged ravine.

In the morning he continued south toward the mountains. He traveled quickly, stopping only to fill his canteen at the two small waterholes he found that day.

Shortly before noon, he stumbled onto a cold campsite. He examined it thoroughly, the way Travis had taught him, and decided that the Crow had stayed there the night before. He searched carefully until he found a small strip of white petticoat that Jennie had torn off and left under a sagebrush. It was a sign from her, a prayer that someone would find it.

The Crow were being unusually careless, and Jeremy guessed that they did not suspect his presence. With renewed vigor, Jeremy trotted south toward the hot summer sun.

As dusk approached that evening, Jeremy spotted eight teepees in the crook of a small river that carved a scar in the dry Pryor Mountains. They were nearly hidden by the heavy-leafed cottonwoods and wild rosebushes.

Jeremy dropped to the ground at the edge of a bluff. He watched the teepees, trying to locate Jennie and waiting for the sun to set. There was no sign of his sister, however. He began to think that he had somehow misread the signs and tracked the wrong Indians.

Just at sunset, Jeremy saw three squaws exit one of the teepees and hold the flap open. Jennie stepped out into the receding light. She was still clad in the petticoat that she had worn only two nights before. Even from the distance, Jeremy could tell that she was tired. That didn't surprise him. She, too, had traveled hard and was probably stiff from being tied up. But at least she was alive and Jeremy thanked the merciful Lord for that small miracle.

The Indian women herded Jennie down to the river behind a thick stand of brambles where he guessed they would bathe. That might be his chance, he thought, possibly his only chance.

If somehow he could quietly lure Jennie away from the women, they might vanish into the trees and be cloaked in the descending night. They could use the dark hours to thread their way out of the river valley and back onto the trail to Fort Stillwater. By hiding during the day and traveling at night, they might elude the Indians long enough to reach Travis and the wagon train.

It was a slim chance, Jeremy knew, but it was their only chance. It was better than the chance that the Blackfoot had given his parents. It was better to die fighting, he decided. It was a good day to die.

Jeremy crawled on his stomach from the bluff to a spot just a few yards downriver from the brambles where the women were bathing. He carefully searched for the lookouts and found none. Jeremy would need the advantage of surprise for his one-man mission. Without that, there was no hope.

From his position on his riverbank, he saw the Indian women splashing about in the water, playing games and laughing. Jennie had secluded herself in a shallow part of the river a few yards away from the other women. She sat quiet and naked as she watched the other women.

Jeremy knew that she was afraid, and he breathed hard. He was frightened, too. He closed his eyes for a moment to reconstruct the vision of his parents lying in the morning grass, scalped and dead. All Indians were savages, he thought, and they would pay. Somehow, they would pay.

He edged close enough to the women until he could see the drops of muddy river water sliding off their straight black hair. Finally, he was only a few yards from Jennie.

He tried to get her attention by doing a very poor bird call. The Indian women were too engrossed in their water games to hear the intruder, but Jennie turned her head. She recognized the bird call from all the hours that they had practiced as they trekked from Missouri.

Jennie gasped and started to call out. Jeremy quickly put his finger to his lips, ordering her to silence. She looked back hastily and watched the three women splashing about and laughing.

For a moment, she was unsure. Then calmly, bravely, Jennie stood up in the shallow water and took a few steps toward the bank. Her immodesty shocked Jeremy. He had never seen his younger sister so naked and white, but he realized that she was trying not to attract attention by feigning modesty.

One of the women turned and yelled at Jennie. Jeremy froze. Jennie calmly picked up her petticoat and squatted on the riverbank. She laid the petticoat across her knees and watched the Indian women. The Indian woman who had yelled at her was eyeing her carefully, but decided nothing was amiss. After a few tense seconds, the woman returned to her playful friends.

Shortly, Jennie stood up and slipped the petticoat over her head. She slid it over her body and brushed it into place. The Indian woman watched her for a moment, but when Jennie squatted again on the bank, the Indian woman went back to her games.

While Jennie was squatting on the riverbank, Jeremy had crawled a few feet closer. He was afraid of being spotted, though, so he kept the wild rosebushes between him and the women. He stopped about twenty yards downstream from where Jennie was sitting and carefully poked his rifle through the brush.

He aimed his long rifle at the woman who had yelled at Jennie—she would be the first to feel his fury. He took a deep breath and glanced quickly at Jennie. She was frantically brushing her hair with her fingers. Jeremy realized that she was signaling him not to shoot.

Jeremy slowly lowered the rifle and Jennie calmed down. Jeremy took a long look around him and realized why Jennie had signaled him. If Jeremy fired the rifle, the warriors would be on him before he ever had a chance to reload or to rescue Jennie. It was less than fifty yards to the teepees. The young warriors were there, always ready for combat with a lone assailant.

He cursed under his breath as he crouched, trying to devise a new plan.

About that time, Jennie stood up and started walking away from him, up the riverbank. She was heading back toward the teepees.

The Indian woman who had yelled before stood up in the water and yelled again. The woman waved at Jennie and called out wildly in her native tongue. Jeremy did not understand her, but he figured that she wanted Jennie to get back to her designated spot on the riverbank. Jennie calmly pointed toward the teepees, took a couple steps and pointed again. The Indian woman looked around at her companions. There was some murmuring among the women but she finally waved her back to the teepees. The women once again returned to their splashing.

Jennie turned toward the camp and started walking up the bank. They were letting her walk the fifty yards back to the teepees alone.

As soon as Jennie entered the heavy brush, she ducked to

the right and started winding her way quietly toward Jeremy. Jeremy moved away from the riverbank, too, and intercepted her.

He grabbed her and hugged her tightly. She was crying.

"Jeremy! I thought you were dead, too. I didn't see you that morning and I knew they got you."

She cried softly as Jeremy cradled her head on his shoulder.

"It's okay, sis. We're together now. Let's get out of here."

"We don't have a chance, Jeremy. There are too many of them."

"Sure, we can make it. I made it here without being spotted so we can make it out just as easy. We'll head for that line of hills, then across the prairie until we meet up with Travis again."

Jennie sniffled.

"Get rid of those tears and let's move. We have to get out of here before the women find that you aren't at the teepees."

Jennie stifled her cry, wiping a tear on the back of her hand.

"We don't have much light left. Pretty soon we won't be able to see where we're going. We've got to get as far away from here as we can or we'll be stuck in the brush all night."

Jeremy and Jennie stole quickly away from the camp, passing like evening shadows through the wild rosebushes and willows. They moved carefully, trying not to rustle the drying grass or snap branches on the scrubby trees. They angled to the west, retracing Jeremy's approach. They dropped to their hands and knees behind a small cutbank that provided the only cover between them and the teepees. They could still see the tops of the teepee poles rising above the grass and scrub bushes.

Suddenly, a shout went up around the camp. A woman screamed and cursed.

The young Missourians lay on their stomachs for a few moments, praying desperately to God for another miracle. Maybe they had not discovered Jennie's escape. Maybe it was something else. Maybe they would look upstream along the riverbank first instead of searching in the thickets. Maybe they would check the other tents first.

But soon Jeremy could hear braves and women running through the grass and brush, fanning out in every direction. His stomach sank as he heard someone running swiftly toward them.

Jeremy turned to meet Jennie's wide eyes.

"They know," she whispered.

"Shut up and crawl faster," Jeremy whispered frantically. "We've got to make it to those trees. Then we'll make a run for it."

They crawled on their stomachs now, trying to move swiftly and secretly through the grass. Jeremy heard the moccasins tearing through the brush on all sides of him now, and he crouched lower.

There was a shout nearby. Jeremy knew that they had spotted Jennie's white petticoat. It was time for battle.

Jeremy heard a shout and saw two young warriors racing headlong toward them. He pulled his rifle up and cocked it. He waited for three eternal seconds until they were almost upon him, then leaped up.

Jeremy jerked the rifle to his shoulder and squeezed the trigger. The explosion belched fire and smoke, obliterating the targets. Both Indians dove to the ground, but the ball never left the rifle. River mud had plugged the barrel. The rifle was destroyed and useless.

The blue smoke drifted peacefully toward the river. The two young Indians looked at each other, dazed but alive.

One of them jumped up and ran shrieking toward Jeremy. In an instant, he reached Jeremy, tomahawk held high and poised for death. Jeremy gripped the rifle by the barrel and the stock. He jammed it above his head as the tomahawk clanged against the metal barrel. Jeremy swung the rifle around and slammed the stock against the side of the Indian's head. He fell stone-like to the ground.

The second Indian was more cautious in his approach now, having no desire to make the same impetuous mistake. He circled the white man carefully, his right arm outstretched with a knife parrying menacingly.

Jeremy grabbed his rifle with both hands on the barrel and took a mighty swing at the Indian. The Indian was too fast. He stepped aside, feigned attack and sliced at Jeremy. Jeremy blocked it with the rifle stock. The Indian sliced again but missed. They circled each other, looking for the advantage.

Jeremy was not trained in this fighting as was his opponent. Only Jeremy's lightning instincts kept the cold steel from piercing his flesh. If he could quickly incapacitate this Indian, he and Jennie might still escape.

Within seconds, though, all hopes of escape evaporated. Jeremy became aware that they were quickly being surrounded. Indians were arriving in twos and threes to form a loose circle that closed off all avenues of escape.

In his mind, there was already a vision of himself lying dead on the ground, bleeding from a knife wound. It was over. He knew it. He could hear Jennie crying behind him. At least, he thought, I want her to remember that I died fighting.

For just another moment, though, he had to stay alive. Jeremy watched the eyes of this young brave. The brave was determined to prove his manhood by killing a white man in hand-to-hand combat. The flicker of hate in the young Indian's eyes sent cold chills through Jeremy. For an instant, he envisioned his own scalp swinging limply from the mane of an Indian horse.

The brave lunged skillfully but Jeremy stepped aside. He swung at the brave with his rifle, but missed, just brushing the top of the grass. With each step, they waited for the other to make a move, a mistake, so this battle could be finalized in blood. They circled cautiously, picking their steps in the dry grass, readying themselves for the final desperate lunge.

Suddenly, a large older Indian stepped from the solid circle of Indians. He yelled something at the young brave. The brave hesitated and looked up, displeased about relinquishing his prey.

The large Indian repeated his warning, this time more insistently. The young Indian begrudgingly stepped back and stabbed his knife into its sheath. He turned toward the teepees and stalked away. The fight was over.

The large Indian approached Jeremy and pointed at the lad's rifle and knife. Jeremy crouched and gripped the broken rifle tightly, ready to defend himself again. The Indian's face showed no signs of sympathy, though, as he pointed to the useless rifle.

Jeremy looked around slowly. There were Indians on all sides of him now. Many were strong young braves armed with bows and arrows, lances or tomahawks. Even the women carried knives in their belts. All weapons were unsheathed and in their hands. The odds were too great. He had no chance now.

He looked at Jennie as she lay crouched in the grass. Her petticoat was clutched tightly around her legs. The Indians stepped between Jeremy and Jennie. She cried hysterically as the women approached her and lifted her up. They had to hold her on her feet.

The first Indian that Jeremy clubbed started to moan, regaining consciousness. No one went to his aid, though. The Indian would someday forget the humiliation of a lost coup. His next attack would be more cautious.

It's over, Jeremy thought, and he dropped his knife and useless rifle into the brittle August grass.

FIVE

Jeremy lay quietly in the teepee. His hands and feet were bound with leather thongs and he was thrown on a pile of foul-smelling buffalo robes. Jennie had been taken away, too. Jeremy didn't know where, but suspected that she was back with the women in another teepee.

A half-dozen Crow were arguing violently outside Jeremy's teepee. There would not be another chance for escape, he knew. They would not let down their guard again.

He cursed his stupidity and foul luck. He had botched the rescue. If the women had not discovered Jennie's absence for a couple more minutes, they would have made it to the hills. Then they could have run. Then they might have had a chance. Getting caught in the middle of the Indian encampment was humiliating for Jeremy. Jennie must think that he was just a dumb kid who almost got them killed with his half-baked plan.

Jeremy did not understand why they allowed him to live. It would have been so easy for the Crow to kill him. An arrow, a knife, a bullet. They had the weapons and the excuse.

The large Indian who broke up the fight was evidently one of the leaders of this small band. He had spoken with the voice of authority and no one questioned his decision to let the young white man live. There had been no discussion, at least in front of the white man.

The Indian wore an otter skin as a headdress so Jeremy decided that he would call him Otter. Otter's face showed years of hardship and battle. He was a powerful man and had obviously earned his position of leadership by strength and wisdom. Jeremy both feared and respected Otter already. Somehow, he must get Otter on his side.

His captors argued fiercely now, though. Jeremy shivered as he remembered the torturous deaths that Travis had told him about during their nights around the campfires. Travis had hissed as he told of men who were tied to trees and used as target practice for young archers. Travis told of a man that he found with a score of rattlesnake bites on his naked body. He had seen men hung upside down in the summer heat, partially eaten by magpies. The only quick death Travis had recounted was a man who was dragged to death behind a horse across the cactus-covered plains.

Jeremy closed his eyes and wished for the horse. It would be fast, at least. He thought of Jennie and what they might decide for her. He shuddered as tears came to his eyes.

Just after dark, Otter stepped into the teepee. An old woman who had been tending the fire slipped quietly outside into the darkness. Jeremy lay still, his hands and feet still tied with sturdy leather thongs.

Otter stood over him, looming in the dancing firelight. Otter lifted his arms to the sky and called upon the Great Spirit for guidance—or at least Jeremy so guessed. Otter was praying in his native Crow, and Jeremy could only surmise what was passing between the Indian and his god.

When Otter finished, he squatted next to Jeremy. Jeremy wiggled, trying to free himself from the leather knots. He twisted and pulled, but the leather only became tighter on his wrists.

Otter spoke firmly to Jeremy, but Jeremy could not understand. He shook his head and shrugged his shoulders.

"I don't understand," he said.

Otter sighed and spoke again, kinder this time. Jeremy still did not understand. Reluctantly, Otter stood up and retreated out the tent flap into the darkness.

Soon the old woman returned with a with a wooden bowl of greasy soup that had lumps of meat and vegetables. She tipped it to Jeremy's lips and he took a mouthful. He winced and spat the broth onto the floor. It was so greasy and salty that he couldn't stomach it. It had been two days since he had eaten much, though, and he knew this was all they had.

The old woman got up to leave but Jeremy called her back. He opened his mouth wide, signaling her to try again. When the old woman tipped the bowl to his lips again, Jeremy took a small sip and swallowed quickly. He shook his head and breathed deep. It was hot, at least, and it would calm the growling in his belly.

The sounds of the camp kept him awake most of the night. He dozed off once and when he awoke, he thought he was back with the wagon train. There was a dog barking, the rustle of someone walking through the grass and the usual night sounds. He heard owls hooting in the cottonwoods and the river tumbling effortlessly over the rocks. Mice and muskrats scampered in the grass and brambles along the river. He heard two male voices talking quietly in the darkness, and for a moment, he was comforted. Then he realized that they were speaking Crow.

In the morning, the argument over Jeremy and Jennie's fate was even more heated. By midmorning, however, Otter had won the approval of the other elders.

Three braves came into the tent and untied Jeremy's legs. With his hands still tied, they led him outside to a horse. Otter and four other braves were already astride their horses. Jennie was there, too. She was mounted on a small roan with her hands tied in front of her. Whatever their fate would be, it would not be here in this camp. With little fanfare, the small band turned and rode out of camp.

The seven horses were driven south that day. It was a long ride for the two young white folks. They were not used to riding all day—they had walked from Missouri. The Indians, however, spent their entire lives on horseback and an all-day ride came naturally to them.

Being tied did not make it easier, either. The rider could not move about much for fear of falling off into the sagebrush and cactus. All they could do was hang on and ride and ride and ride.

By dark, Jeremy was riding limply with his head down when he heard Jennie catch a quick breath. He looked up to find themselves on top of a ridge overlooking a river valley. Although the winding river valley was blanketed with cottonwoods, Jeremy could see more than a hundred teepees. He knew that there were more hidden by the sprawling cottonwoods.

The first camp where they had been captured was evidently just a hunting party for this larger band. Once they got into this camp of hundreds of teepees and warriors, there would never again be a chance for escape.

Jeremy looked around hurriedly, hoping for a last minute chance to escape. It was impossible, though, because the Indians already realized it, too. Their lances were poised on their captives. Even if Jeremy could surprise them and make a run for it, Jennie would never be able to follow. He had to wait. He had no choice.

When the five Indians paraded into the large Crow village with two white hostages, there was a sudden bustle of excitement. Women and children flocked from their teepees to see and touch these unusual light-skinned people. The white men had been in this part of the Upper Great Plains for some forty years but these isolated bands of roving Crow seldom saw them. For some of the younger children, this was their first encounter with white people.

The children followed the horses closely and tried to touch Jeremy and Jennie on the legs. Jennie's bare legs hung below her petticoat and down within their reach. The children giggled at the strangers and tried to feel the soft white petticoat. She tried to pull her legs up from their curious fingers, but nearly slipped off her horse.

The seven riders pulled up in front of a large red teepee. Otter shouted at the red teepee and a well-built warrior stepped into the dimming light. This was Braids His Hair On Top, chief of this band of Crow.

Otter and the warrior raised their arms in greeting. Otter spoke to the warrior for a few moments, and the warrior's eyes grew large. Jeremy moved back on his horse, fearing the sinister expression. Braids His Hair On Top stepped toward Jeremy and looked him over, then glanced briefly at the young white girl. Satisfied, he retreated to the red teepee.

Jeremy looked over at Jennie, "For some reason, they're more interested in me than you."

"I don't understand it either, Jeremy. They were so calm and quiet until yesterday when you arrived. Then the whole camp was fighting over you. It was like half the camp wanted to kill you and the other half thought you were their savior. It's all so strange."

"Looks like we'll find out pretty soon," Jeremy said as Braids His Hair On Top stepped out of the red teepee, followed by a small wiry Indian. The old man's white hair hung in braids over his chest and he wore a buckskin shirt that was beaded simply with shells and porcupine quills. The deerhide shirt was shiny with grease and age. Many of the long fringes had been cut or torn so that only a few long tassels remained.

The old man hobbled up to Jeremy's horse and said something to Otter. Otter took his lance and poked Jeremy in the side, repeating the old man's words. Jeremy didn't understand, but when Otter poked him again with the steel-tipped lance, Jeremy slid down off his horse. That was evidently all the old man had wanted.

He circled Jeremy slowly, carefully eyeing him, as if sizing him up for a marriage to his granddaughter. Jeremy trembled slightly.

The old man mumbled and touched Jeremy's arms, rubbing slightly as if to make sure that he was indeed white. He walked up to Otter who was still mounted on his horse and said a few words. Otter nodded and signaled to the other riders. The four other riders rode quickly out of camp and to the north, leaving Otter and the captives.

Jeremy somehow knew that he now belonged to this old man. He was confused. The Crow captured women to be their slaves, not men. Why did this old man want Jeremy?

The old man returned to his teepee and two armed braves escorted Jeremy and Jennie into a nearby teepee. They were placed on opposite sides of the teepee on buffalo robes and their feet were bound again. The braves left but an old woman stayed with them, sewing a rabbitskin in the corner. Jeremy could hear them talking as they stood guard at the tent flap.

After days of hard riding and running, Jeremy could not even consider another escape attempt. This Crow village was too large, too spread out. And he was simply too exhausted.

"Are you okay, Jennie?" he asked finally, peering across the dim light to the other pile of buffalo robes.

"I think so. I'm so tired. I can't ride anymore. My tailbone hurts so bad."

"Yeah. Mine, too."

A while later, Jeremy ventured a thought, "Shall we try to get out of here?"

Jennie shook her head.

"No, I can't. I'm so tired that I couldn't run even if I was untied. Besides, there's hundreds of them. We don't have a rifle or even a knife. It's at least three days ride to the wagon train, even if we could get horses and didn't get lost."

Jeremy swallowed.

"I hate it when you're right. We'll just have to wait. At

least it doesn't look like they're going to kill us. They seem to want me for something."

They were silent for a time. They could hear the laughter of children as they played outside the teepee. The women giggled as they gossiped around the cooking pots. Jeremy closed his eyes and once again, it was like being back with the wagon train.

"They really have been good to me," Jennie said. "The women don't let the young braves come near me. They fed me, even if it was that greasy soup and buffalo jerky. I know it's the same thing they eat."

"I know. I wish I could think of some way to escape. But I'm so tired, too."

The morning sun was well into the eastern sky before anyone else came to check on the captives. There was a lot of activity in camp, but there were no arguments like in the small camp. It was all very normal for a morning in the Crow camp.

Another old woman came in to feed Jeremy and Jennie the greasy stew that they were becoming accustomed to. This time, however, there was a bowl of pulverized berries too, a piece of rock-hard buffalo jerky and a very mild tea, probably made of rosehips.

Shortly after they finished eating, an unusual looking Indian entered the teepee. He barked at the old woman and she slipped away through the tent flap.

The man was not dressed like the other Crow men. His brown corduroy pants were probably brought up on one of the steamboats that plied the Yellowstone River. He wore a faded torn cavalry shirt that was decorated with porcupine quills and trade beads, and calf-high moccasin style boots. His black braids fell out of a wide-brimmed, flat-topped felt hat like those worn by the white settlers and river people. He had obviously been to the trading posts along the Yellowstone River.

He pounded his chest and stood tall. "Crazy Bear."

Jeremy and Jennie looked at each other in surprise. Although he probably did not speak much English, at least he knew some. Maybe he could tell them what was going on. Maybe he knew why the old man had such an interest in Jeremy.

Jeremy summed up all his courage and said to Crazy Bear, "I am Jeremy. This is Jennie, my sister."

Crazy Bear pointed to them in order, "Jeremy. Sister."

Jeremy looked at Jennie. It really didn't make that much difference that he didn't catch her name, they guessed.

"Why are we being kept here?" Jeremy asked Crazy Bear. "We want to go back to our wagon train."

Crazy Bear shook his head.

"You stay. Medicine Elk need Jeremy for trip to mountain. You stay two suns, then go with Medicine Elk to mountain."

"Who is Medicine Elk?" Jeremy asked.

"Medicine Elk, old man, red teepee. He save your life. He dream about you. You come to him like dream says. You stay and take him to mountain."

"I don't want to go with Medicine Elk. Just let us go. Me and my sister."

"No. You go mountain."

With that, Crazy Bear quickly turned and exited through the tent flap. Jeremy and Jennie were stunned.

"What was he talking about?" Jeremy asked.

"I'm not sure," Jennie answered quietly.

Jeremy pondered Crazy Bear's words for a while.

Finally, he said, "That's why they didn't kill me. This Medicine Elk dreamed about me."

"What about this mountain?" Jennie asked.

"I don't have all the answers yet, Jennie. But at least I know why Otter stopped them from killing me."

"Who's Otter?"

"One of the leaders. The one that stopped the fight. He wears an otter skin headdress."

Jennie nodded. "I know him. He's the one that…"

A half-dozen braves burst through the tent flap. They grabbed Jeremy and lifted him up roughly. They cut the leather thongs on his feet and pushed him toward the tent flap.

"I think I'm about to find out," he told Jennie as he stumbled through the tent flap. "Wish me luck."

"Good luck," she called after him.

Jeremy was escorted to the red teepee. One brave opened the tent flap while another pushed him through the opening. Jeremy entered cautiously and stood up in the smoky lodge. Eight older Indians sat in a half-circle around the smoldering fire. The acrid smoke rose slowly to the opening in the blackened top of the teepee.

Jeremy recognized four of the Indians. Crazy Bear was there, probably as interpreter. The old man, Medicine Elk, was seated in the back, partially obscured by the smoke. On Medicine Elk's right side sat Otter and Braids His Hair On Top.

Crazy Bear looked up at Jeremy and motioned for him to sit on a trade blanket on the far left side of the half-circle. Clumsily, Jeremy sat down and surveyed the Crow warriors.

Jeremy remembered Travis's stories about the Indians who would cut off one of their finger joints in commemoration of one of their dead relatives. A few of these Crow had the short fingers that Travis had told him about. Medicine Elk was missing part of three fingers and Jeremy wondered for which relatives he had cut them off.

For a long time, no one spoke. Medicine Elk rocked back and forth in his cross-legged position, sometimes singing softly, other times silent. The other seven warriors watched him intently, quietly, as if they were waiting for the Great Spirit to speak through him.

Jeremy wanted to ask Crazy Bear more questions but decided to wait. Breaking Medicine Elk's trancelike state would be a violation of some unspoken Crow law. He would not risk their anger. Jeremy decided to wait.

In time, Medicine Elk stopped rocking and singing. He opened his eyes. He looked around as if he was surprised to find anyone else in the teepee with him. When he spotted Jeremy, an alien, he eyed him closely as if he had never seen him before. Then a look of recognition crossed his face and he smiled. He nodded in Jeremy's direction and spoke in Crow.

Crazy Bear began to translate.

"Medicine Elk say you are white man that he saw in his dream in the Winter of the Long Snows. You came with others. They are gone now. You are alone."

"I have my sister," Jeremy interrupted.

Medicine Elk stopped momentarily, surprised at the impertinence of the young man. Crazy Bear said a few quick words to Medicine Elk, calming him.

"White girl not yours. She belong to great Crow warrior. You are alone."

"But she's my sister!"

"She stay with us until you come back from mountain. Then you and Sister together."

Jeremy still wasn't sure what this trip was all about, but he did not like the idea of leaving Jennie with the Crow again. Sure, they hadn't hurt her, but she belonged at the fort or on the wagon train. She didn't belong with these Crow.

Through the translating tongue of Crazy Bear, Medicine Elk started a long rambling story about his life. He told of the winter when the snow had been belly deep on their horses. The cold wind from the north had frozen many of the old people. Some of the children had gotten lost in the snowdrifts along the river and died.

His people had been dying from the evils that the white man had already brought to them. The red fever that came with blankets killed his wife and parents many years ago on the River That Roars Quietly. Jeremy guessed that this was probably the Missouri. Travis had told him about the smallpox that had killed many Indians in the Dakota Territory when the fur traders were just penetrating the area. Jeremy's heart went out to Medicine Elk.

There had been battles with the white people. The Sioux and Blackfoot who had killed his people. Medicine Elk lifted his beaded deerhide vest to show two knife scars and a bullet hole from the battles he had fought.

Jeremy noticed that Medicine Elk had three stub fingers on his left hand. Here was an Indian with short fingers, just like

Travis had said. Each stub meant the loss of a relative or close friend in battle. Medicine Elk's body bore the permanent reminders of the loss of his family and friends.

On his shortened fingers, Medicine Elk counted the coup he had claimed in the forays against the mighty Blackfoot and against the Sioux in the Sacred Hills to the east. He told a story about a horse he had freed from the quicksand in the River That Flows Sand. He trained it to become a warrior's horse. That would be the Black Hills and the Powder River, Jeremy figured.

At last, Medicine Elk's story came to the Winter of Long Snows and how he had dreamed of the young white man. There had been little to eat for two moons because they had eaten their store of dried berries and buffalo fat called pemmican. There were few animals left in the river valley. When one hunter downed a deer with a bow and arrow, all the women came to butcher the carcass and divide the meat among all the families. Because he had no woman, Medicine Elk was often forgotten.

The younger ones ate first, knowing that they needed the strength to hunt more food. The ancient ones waited, however, knowing that their worth had been reduced by age. Slowly, painfully and quietly, each was willing to sacrifice his own life so the tribe might survive until the plentiful spring.

Jeremy winced when Crazy Bear spoke these words. The old people put the survival of the tribe above their own life. They did not expect the tribe to starve on their behalf. Each must contribute to the tribe's welfare. As always, it was their own choice not to eat.

In this period of fasting, Medicine Elk's dream came to him. It was a bitter cold day of brilliant sunshine in the Second Moon of No Food. He had walked upriver until the sun was high, intent on losing himself in the snow. He would not be a burden to the tribe anymore.

He had traveled for many hours when he lay down to die. Then his vision came.

It was a young man, a young white man, like one that Medicine Elk had seen at a trading post along the River of

Yellow Rocks when the beaver men were here. In the dream, the young white man came to Medicine Elk and took his hand. The young white man said that they would go to the mountain together when the ground was warm and the rivers were running again.

The young white man had said, "We will go to the mountain where the wind is fast and keeps us warm. You will not die in the snow, where you will be cold forever. You will be lifted to the sky at sunrise on a platform. You will die in the brown grass when it is warm. You cannot die here. Your spirit cannot rise out of the snow. Your body must start its journey on a platform."

Medicine Elk's memory was blurry. Over the spring and summer, he had added much to the dream.

"You must go back to the village and live until the flowers come and the deer bring small ones onto the grass. You will die with honor worthy of a great warrior of the Crow people. Your spirit will be lifted to the sky at sunrise to start you on the long journey to the place where the buffalo are many and fat, and the winter storms bring only enough snow to track the rabbits and the deer, and the clear cold waters come from the mountains during the summer moons."

Medicine Elk halted, exhausted by the retelling of his dream. The instrument of fulfillment was here now. It was embodied in this young white man who sat with him in the smoky lodge.

It was the beginning of a new life, he knew, and not the end. This was only another journey, except this one would be more difficult because he must pass through an opening in the sky from which there is no return. His father and grandfather had passed through that same opening in the sky before him, but they did not come back to guide him. He must do it alone. There was no one to give advice, just as he could not give advice to his own sons when it came time for them to journey through the opening in the sky.

For the first time, Jeremy understood. He was not saved from death by the knife to be tortured or killed. The Crow would not take revenge on him because other white people were invading the Crow territory. Nor was he brought to this Crow village to be made a slave.

He was brought here to perform a heroic task for this Crow warrior. He was brought here to complete a mission, a mission that was beyond his comprehension. His duty had become the unspeakable task of taking a dying warrior to the mountain where he would die and be lifted to the sky on a platform of limbs and grasses. He must lift this Crow to the sky at sunrise and help him through the hole in the sky.

There was no animosity against him in this group, he realized. Rather, he was accepted because of Medicine Elk's dream. Without Jeremy, the soul of the warrior Medicine Elk would not rest peacefully.

Jeremy was scared, petrified, because he knew that he could not do it. He had left his own parents unburied on the prairie because he could not bear the thought of touching their cold bodies. He could not place them in the Christian graves that his own culture dictated.

He wondered, too, if he would be allowed to return from the mountain once Medicine Elk's body had been raised. The thought of Jennie living with the Crow forever tore at his heart.

"Crazy Bear," he said at last in desperation, "he cannot think that I am the white man that he dreamed about. I am too young. It should be an older white man, one that is stronger than me. I am too small to lift him onto the platform. I can't do it, Crazy Bear, I can't do it."

There was a tear forming in the corner of Jeremy's eye. He could see that Crazy Bear was listening to him, but was not hearing his words. Crazy Bear did not translate Jeremy's words to Medicine Elk. He didn't need to. Everyone understood him already.

There were a few moments of desperate silence. Medicine Elk and Jeremy studied each other. Jeremy's lower lip quivered and he thought he would panic. Again, he saw the bloodied bodies of his own parents lying motionless in the burning grass. He couldn't touch them.

Crazy Bear spoke a few words to Medicine Elk. There was a pause and Medicine Elk replied in only a short phrase.

Crazy Bear turned to Jeremy and said, "I asked Medicine Elk if he was sure that you are the white man in his dream. He say, 'yes, you are the one.'"

"No, I can't be, Crazy Bear. Tell him he is wrong. Tell him that he dreamed wrong!"

Crazy Bear shook his head slowly. "Medicine Elk always dreams strange. They always come true. At first, we laughed at his dreams. Now, no laugh. He dream of white people before beaver men. He dream of teepees on wheels pulled by many horses. Then they came. We afraid. We remembered Medicine Elk's dream."

He continued, "First, only some on the big river. Medicine Elk dream they are grasshoppers and cover us. We laughed. Now, no laugh. Now, more wagons than grasshoppers on the road at the big river."

Jeremy pleaded, "I could go away. I could go back to the east, where the white people live, and I would never come back."

Crazy Bear shook his head again. "You no understand. You go back, wagons do not stop. Is no last wagon. You dead now if Medicine Elk did not dream you here. Medicine Elk have powerful dreams. No warrior will fight his medicine dreams. Medicine Elk dreamed right. You go to mountain."

Jeremy choked back a sob and wiped a budding tear before the warriors could see it trickle down his cheek. He took a deep breath and closed his eyes. They were seeing his weakness, he knew, but the mission overwhelmed him. After a moment, he opened them and looked at Crazy Bear.

"Tell me what I must do."

Crazy Bear said something again to Medicine Elk, and Medicine Elk smiled a long toothless smile. Jeremy would have smiled, too, except that fright gripped his thoughts.

"Today, you go to mountain," said Crazy Bear. "Follow Medicine Elk to high ground. You take jerky and water for you. Medicine Elk no eat, no drink."

"Do we go alone?" Jeremy asked. In the back of his mind, he thought that he might leave Medicine Elk or even kill him, and then return to Jennie.

Crazy Bear knew his thoughts, though, because the elders had decided they could not trust any white man, even the one in Medicine Elk's dream.

"Two Crow warriors will follow. You not see them. They watch from faraway that you raise Medicine Elk to the sky like dream. When done, you return. We give horses and food. You leave village. Go east, go west, go to wagons."

"How far is this mountain?" Jeremy asked softly, slowly regaining his confidence.

"Four, five suns to the west. Medicine Elks knows."

Jeremy conceded.

"Tell Medicine Elk I will do it. I will take him to the mountain."

Crazy Bear looked toward Medicine Elk and just nodded. The other warriors smiled briefly, then one of the more battle-scarred warriors lit the pipe of peace. The pipe was passed around the half-circle. The ritual of trust was performed.

Each man presented the pipe to each of the four winds, took a shallow puff, and passed the pipe to the next man. When it came Jeremy's turn, he followed suit and performed the ritual in the same manner. They had offered him his life in return for completing this unusual mission. And he had accepted them.

Crazy Bear offered Jeremy a steel-bladed knife and tomahawk.

"You need at mountain."

"For what?"

"Medicine Elk tell you."

"But I do not speak Crow."

"He tell you with his heart."

When the meeting was finished, the Indians and Jeremy stood up and filed out of the tent, all except for Medicine Elk. He remained seated and reverted to his trancelike state of rocking back and forth singing.

When they stepped into the bright sun again, Jeremy asked Crazy Bear, "When do I leave?"

"You leave before sun dies. You get food, water now. When Medicine Elk comes out of lodge, you leave."

"Can I see my sister before I go?"

Crazy Bear shrugged his shoulders. "Yes, but be ready."

With that, Jeremy hurried to the lodge where Jennie was being kept. A young brave who was guarding the prisoner stepped into Jeremy's path as he approached the lodge, but Jeremy strode up to him. He looked the brave directly in the eyes. Without words, the brave knew that Jeremy was now part of Medicine Elk's dream. The brave stepped aside and allowed Jeremy to enter Jennie's teepee.

Jennie was surprised to see Jeremy.

"You're back," she gasped.

Jeremy nodded, "But I have to leave."

"You have to take me with you. You can't leave me here."

"I'm not going back to the wagons, Jennie. I have to take an old Indian warrior to the mountain where he will die."

"What?"

Jeremy quickly cut Jennie's leather thongs to free her.

"I don't have time to explain it all, but the old medicine man dreamed that a young white man would take him to the mountain and raise his body to the sky at sunrise. That young man is me, I guess. He dreamed about me. It's crazy, but it's the only way I can see to get us out of here."

"When will you be back to get me?"

"In a week or so. I have to wait for him to die. But they said that when I returned from the mountain, you and I are free to leave. We can catch another wagon train on the Bozeman Trail and go on to Fort Stillwater. From there we'll make some other plans. But I have to make this journey with Medicine Elk first."

"What if something happens and you don't come back?"

Jeremy shuddered. "I don't know."

SIX

Jeremy was ready. The women brought him a soft rawhide pack with beef jerky and pemmican and a buffalo bladder of water. They gave him a large steel knife that he strapped to his belt, then squatted in the shade to wait. He asked to see Jennie again but they refused him. They did not want him to change his mind.

Shortly after the heat of the day, Medicine Elk hobbled out of the teepee. He straightened up, high and proud for a moment, before slumping back down to his aged posture. He looked at Jeremy and without speaking, moved slowly out of camp.

Medicine Elk and Jeremy headed due west, toward the setting sun and the mountains that separated the deep blue sky from the dry brown prairie. The mountains were a refuge. They were cool in the summer with crystalline streams tumbling from the sheltered snowbanks that never quite melted from year to year. The tall pines tamed the winter winds and softened the summer thunderstorms. To look to the mountains was to see peace.

Jeremy knew that they would not travel to the farthest or highest peak. Such a journey was beyond the strength and skill of both of them, especially Medicine Elk. Jeremy knew it as well as the old man. Jeremy figured that they would hike into the high country and pick a promontory point with a spectacular view of the valleys. They would settle there for Medicine Elk's death ritual.

Jeremy was surprised at the speed with which they traveled through the open grasslands. Despite his ancient body, Medicine Elk had been hardened by decades of walking. He had walked and ridden for days on end, moving from one camp to another or trailing the buffalo, elk and deer. Now, too, he had a purpose in life again.

Jeremy had two things in his favor, however, that allowed him to keep up with Medicine Elk. First, his youth gave him the strength and a great reserve of endurance. Second, his own body was lean and refined from the long walk from Missouri. He felt physically prepared for this short trip.

They stopped shortly before sunset, already covering a good ten miles. Jeremy spotted a clump of chokecherry bushes in a dry ravine and pointed them out to Medicine Elk. Medicine Elk did not speak, but changed his course toward the bushes. They sat down next to the chokecherries to rest.

Medicine Elk crossed his legs and closed his eyes. Within a couple minutes, he had slipped into his trancelike meditation. He sang and hummed until he was oblivious to his surroundings. He must prepare himself for his death.

Jeremy moved away from Medicine Elk, not wanting to disturb him. He picked and ate some of the bitter purple chokecherries, spitting out as many of the small seeds as he could. The ripe berries made his lips pucker, but at least it was different than the jerky in his pack.

As it grew darker, Jeremy returned to Medicine Elk and sat

near him. He pulled out a strip of deer jerky and gnawed on it. He thought about his mother's wonderful meals in their Missouri home and wished this food was softer and more palatable. The jerky was too tough to be a pleasant meal, but it did stifle the hunger in his stomach. Jeremy knew that tomorrow would be another full day of hiking as Medicine Elk pushed on to the west.

With the last piece of jerky still unchewed in his mouth, Jeremy lay back on the grass and dozed off. Medicine Elk finished his moaning chant long after dark and Jeremy, in exhaustion, drifted off to sleep.

The next day they entered more rugged terrain. The grassland slowly gave way to the foothills of the mountains. The foothills were little more than a series of long rough ridges that sported clumps of scraggly pine trees, twisted juniper bushes, a few yucca and scattered chokecherries. There was not enough rain in these foothills. The grass and trees hugged the bottoms of the ravines where the moisture trickled down the slopes to concentrate in the shade. Both Jeremy and Medicine Elk slipped and stumbled on the rocks.

Jeremy kept watching behind them. He hoped to catch a glimpse of the two braves that were supposed to be following them. In two days, he never saw them. He began to wonder if maybe the council had deceived him. Maybe they told him about two imaginary braves just to keep him from abandoning Medicine Elk. Maybe it was a trick to prevent him from killing the old Indian so he could return to the village sooner to retrieve Jennie.

Jeremy pondered that for a long time as they struggled through the foothills. In his head, he tried to develop ways for Medicine Elk to die. Jeremy thought about doing it by his own hand, but wasn't sure that he could shed the old man's blood. He devised an imaginary rockslide, but in his heart, he knew that he would still have to finish off the Indian. Either way, though, he could return to the village to say that Medicine Elk was now with the Great Spirit.

Besides the act of murder, the other problem was that the

Crow did not expect Jeremy to return so soon. Everyone knew that it should take four or five days for Medicine Elk to give up his life. Jeremy would have to wait a few days before completing the grisly task.

Besides, if the two braves really were following him, they would discover his treachery. They would easily outrun him back to the village. Then, Jennie would have no chance of returning to the white people. Jeremy, too, could never risk entering the Crow camp again. Maybe he would actually have to wait for Medicine Elk to die according to the plan the Great Spirit had anointed for him.

They spent the second night curled up under a small rock overhang among a stand of tall pines on the south side of a rocky hillside. He ate more of the jerky but it did little to ease his hunger from the strenuous traveling. There was very little natural food in these barren foothills so he settled for jerky.

All during those two days, Medicine Elk did not eat or drink. He was on his final fast, Jeremy told himself, just like Crazy Bear had told him. Jeremy once offered Medicine Elk a drink of tepid water. Medicine Elk looked right through the young white man and refused to acknowledge the offer. From then on, Jeremy kept the food and water to himself.

According to the ritual that Medicine Elk had designed, he spent much of his rest time in his meditation and praying. He chanted and hummed, rocking back and forth. Jeremy usually wandered off while Medicine Elk meditated.

It gave him time to think about Jennie. She would be thinking of him too, he knew, and praying to the good Lord that he would return safely. Then, they could go on to Fort Stillwater.

He prayed too, even though sometimes he wondered if it would do any good. Once he wondered whether it was he or Medicine Elk who was praying to the one and only God, and which one of them was being the fool.

By the third morning, Jeremy had convinced himself they were not being followed. It had all been a trick by the Crow so he would follow Medicine Elk through these tough days. He was sure that he could kill or abandon the old man soon. Jeremy decided that Medicine Elk would die tomorrow. He would then return after being gone for six days. That was long enough.

Jeremy planned all day. Medicine Elk was oblivious to the fate that Jeremy had decided for him. Again, he spent the evening in his chanting and meditating. Although Jeremy devised many plans for Medicine Elk's death, most of them lacked either believability or the ease of execution.

In the end, Jeremy decided on the simplest, most direct plan. The complicated arrangements left too much room for error. If his motives were discovered, Medicine Elk might somehow disarm his entire plan.

Jeremy decided finally that a blow to the skull would be best. There were many turtle-sized rocks littering the slopes. They were handy and effective weapons. Jeremy considered his plan carefully. It did not require much cooperation. It could be done in a stand of trees or at the bottom of a coulee for protection against voyeurs. It would be fast and painless for both Jeremy and Medicine Elk.

He would not need to hurry tomorrow, though. In fact, it might be better to wait until later in the evening. Then Medicine Elk's body could be hidden by the darkness for a few hours while he hastily started to the camp where Jennie was being held. He might be able to get enough of a head start so that the two Indians could not catch him—that is, if they were actually following him.

Jeremy watched carefully all day. He hoped to glimpse something that would indicate they were indeed being followed. Everything was quiet, though. He had seen no traces of humans since they left camp. Jeremy even backtracked once as Medicine Elk meditated, but he failed to find any tracks behind them. It was as if he and Medicine Elk were the only people on earth.

He had no doubts now. They were alone. He could carry out his plan without fear of reprisal. Tomorrow Medicine Elk would die.

The sun was bright in the western sky on that third afternoon.

Jeremy became more uneasy as the day wore on. He was plagued by anxiety. He had never killed a man before. Once before in the Crow camp, he thought he might be able to do it. But that would have been to defend his own life. This was murder.

He felt he was being watched. He sensed their presence, but could not see them. They were running away from him, yet chasing him.

Jeremy slept fitfully that night. When he finally woke with a start that morning, the sun had not touched the horizon. The foothills were lit by only the softest pre-dawn light. Jeremy shivered in the cool air. He sat up, stretched himself and moved toward the dead fire.

What he saw made him take a sharp breath. A dead rabbit lay by the cooling embers of the night's fire, its furry body cold and lifeless. The rabbit had a neat hole in its side, pierced by an arrow. A slit ran along the stomach where the insides had been neatly removed. The rabbit had been left for him because his food supply was running low.

"Oh, my God," he whispered to himself. "They're here."

He whirled around quickly, half expecting to see them standing at the edge of his small camp. But the ridges were empty and the horizon told no tale of the night spirits' whereabouts. They had come and gone as quietly as a wisp of campfire smoke. They left only the rabbit and a couple moccasin tracks near the fire where stealth was more important than tracks. Once the tracks left the center of camp, they too disappeared.

The two Indians were following him. They were close enough to know that his food supply was already low.

Jeremy closed his eyes and took a deep breath. He could not kill Medicine Elk. He could not sidestep his mission. The spies were more than his imagination.

Medicine Elk led the way that day, as he had led for three days already. They were well into the high country now, and the land was rugged. There were more chokecherry and buffaloberry bushes in the coulees that tore deeper through the scarred plateau. Tracks of deer and elk were plentiful. Occasionally, they would cross a trail of mangled earth and vegetation where a small herd of bison had passed before them.

As they traveled, Jeremy watched carefully. He surveyed the hillsides on his flanks and the ridges behind him, trying to spot the braves. Twice, he ducked out of sight behind chokecherry bushes and waited for many minutes to see if they would venture from their protective cover, but to no avail. He never saw them, but he felt their presence more strongly now. They were near him, but invisible.

That afternoon, Jeremy and Medicine Elk stopped on a hillside to regain their sapping strength. The long arduous walk was showing on Medicine Elk. His eyes were dimmer now and his pace had slowed. Jeremy wondered if they would ever reach the mountain country that Medicine Elk was watching. Their days of traveling did not seem to bring it much closer.

Jeremy was glad for the rest, though, and glad to see that Medicine Elk was tiring. Each hour Medicine Elk strode forward took Jeremy that much farther from Jennie. It would take that many more hours to return to the Crow encampment on the river. He realized that, even if he saved his strength, it would take three days to get back to Jennie. He wondered if he would ever see her alive again.

Medicine Elk rested for quite a while. While he chanted his dying song, Jeremy lay back in the warm sun. He closed his eyes. He was tired, so tired.

There were only the soft prairie sounds for a long time. The meadowlark chirrahlupped nearby and the afternoon breeze kicked up a small cloud of dust from a buffalo wallow in the bottom of a coulee.

In time, Medicine Elk's chant was complete and he sat quietly. He tilted his head back to the sky and closed his eyes in peacefulness.

Suddenly, there was the sound of horses and Jeremy looked up to see a column of blue-coated soldiers topping the ridge opposite them. They trotted down the long slope and through the sparse grass at the bottom of the coulee. The soldiers had seen the two lone wanderers and were moving in to investigate. Upon seeing that one of them was a white man, they spurred their horses to a run. They hoped to arrive before the Indian had a chance to overpower the white man.

Jeremy was stunned. I'm being rescued, he thought. But, God, they can't rescue me yet!

He leaped to his feet and prayed that the two Indian scouts had not seen the horse-soldiers. He grabbed Medicine Elk by the arm and pulled him up.

"Let's go," he yelled. "We have to go now."

Jeremy pulled at Medicine Elk as they stumbled up the hill away from the cavalry troops. It was no use. The soldiers were galloping and there was no cover. There were no bushes on this hillside and even if there were, it was too late to hide. They were being rescued—or captured. Jeremy wasn't sure.

"Hold up," came the cry from the front rider.

Jeremy looked around and realized the fruitlessness of flight. He stopped, trying to formulate some excuse to give the cavalry. He knew what they would say. They would want to know why he was wandering around this desolation with an old Indian. Where did he come from? He couldn't be out here alone. It wouldn't make sense to them.

Within seconds, the cavalry had reined their horses up to within a few yards of Jeremy and Medicine Elk. Jeremy looked furtively at the twenty-some soldiers, each packing a rifle, a sidearm and enough ammunition for a small battle. He could see that they were restless and tired, too, because they had been on the trail for a few days.

The front rider, a lieutenant, leaned forward on his sweating horse.

"Who are you, boy?"

Jeremy didn't answer right away. All he could see in his mind's eye was two scouts retreating to the Crow camp with news of Medicine Elk's capture. He would never see Jennie again.

"Answer me, boy. Indians cut out your tongue?"

"Uh, no, sir. Umm, my name's Jeremy Higgins from Missouri."

The man gave Jeremy a long cold stare.

"You're a long ways from Missouri, boy."

"Yes, sir."

"Did you say Higgins?" he repeated. "You Thomas Higgins's boy?"

Jeremy knew now that these men were scouring the countryside looking for him and Jennie. His friend Travis had somehow alerted the cavalry at Fort Stillwater and these men were here to rescue him from the savages.

"Uh, yes, sir. He's dead, though."

The lieutenant straightened up in his saddle and took a deep breath.

"I know, boy. Fella named Travis buried him on the Bozeman Trail a few days ago."

The words rang in Jeremy's ears. Travis's final words to them had come true. He had buried Thomas Higgins.

The lieutenant continued, "He couldn't find you or the girl so he figured you musta been taken prisoner. Looks like he was right."

"I'm not a prisoner, sir. This Indian was showing me back to the trail so I could catch another wagon train."

The lieutenant smiled down at Jeremy.

"You've been going the wrong way for a long time then, son. You ain't even close to the trail anymore."

Jeremy thought quickly. He couldn't let them take Medicine Elk. Medicine Elk was on his death journey. They couldn't take him back to the fort.

"Well, that's okay, I guess. Now that you're here, I'll just go with you."

Jeremy quickly turned away from Medicine Elk and walked up to the blue-coated soldiers.

"Which of the men do I ride with, sir?"

"You can ride with the sergeant there. The Indian'll have to walk. Corporal, tie the Injun's hands together and trail him behind you."

Fear stabbed at Jeremy. They were taking Medicine Elk prisoner. Jeremy could not let the Indian scouts see their brethren tied and trailed away. They would assume that

Medicine Elk would be killed. They would know that he died an indignant and humiliating death at the hands of the treacherous white man.

"No, you can't do that," Jeremy cried out. "He's an old man and he can't walk that far. He'll die."

"You're right," the lieutenant said. "We'll just take care of him here."

He turned around in his saddle.

"Corporal, shoot him."

The corporal immediately pulled his army revolver from his holster and leveled it at Medicine Elk. Medicine Elk stood there quietly, unflinching, seemingly oblivious of his fate.

"No!" screamed Jeremy as he raced in front of Medicine Elk. Jeremy stood full in front of Medicine Elk.

"You can't shoot him, you can't. I need him. I've got to keep him alive so they don't kill my sister."

Jeremy gulped. That was it. The corporal lowered his gun slowly. The lieutenant gave Jeremy a long cold stare.

"Corporal, holster that pistol." Then he turned to Jeremy.

"We're all going back to the fort, boy. You can ride double with that Injun if you want. But don't try anything funny. I don't want to shoot a white man, especially a boy."

Jeremy knew what the lieutenant meant. Any false move would lead to Medicine Elk's instant death. Plus, he would be tied to his horse for the ride back to Fort Stillwater. There was a hard quality about this cavalry man that frightened Jeremy and heightened his desperation to escape.

One of the soldiers dismounted and handed the reins to Jeremy. Quickly, the soldier mounted up double with another soldier. Jeremy mounted into the stiff cavalry saddle and nudged the horse over to where Medicine Elk stood.

He held his hand down to Medicine Elk. The Indian looked up at the young white man with saddened eyes. There was a pause before the recognition. Medicine Elk knew his ensuing fate, and in his stoic manner, had accepted that fate. He was too old to fight.

Medicine Elk reached up and grasped Jeremy's hand.

Jeremy hoisted him up into the saddle behind him. With a hard nudge to the flanks, Jeremy turned the horse and fell in with the soldiers as they headed for Fort Stillwater.

They had been riding only a few minutes when two cavalry scouts came galloping up, their horses heaving from a hard ride. The two men pulled their horses to a halt that raised a billowing cloud of dust that choked Jeremy. He blinked his eyes hard to rid them of the dust.

The older man, a corporal, raised a black, hairy thing in his hand and waved it at the troops.

"I got one, Lieutenant, I got one."

The younger soldier yelled too, "He did, sir. He shot that thievin' Injun."

Jeremy was aghast. As the soldier waved the hairy black scalp over his head, droplets of fresh blood spattered to the ground and down the man's tanned arm. It was a fresh scalp with the rawhide thongs still tying the two braids together.

Jeremy swallowed hard. He closed his eyes and his head fell forward on his chest. It was over now, he knew.

"What the devil are you talking about, corporal?" the lieutenant commanded sharply. "Slow down and start talking sense."

"Yessir," the corporal replied quickly. "Well, McCormick and me, we seen these two Injuns over on that ridge in some scrub trees," he said as he pointed to the east. "They was a-watching you take that old Injun and kid and didn't see us at all. We sneaked up on 'em and I got one of 'em. McCormick only winged his and he got away, but we sure took care of this one."

He proudly held up the bloody scalp.

"Corporal, you're going on report for this," the lieutenant snapped. "Colonel Whitney has specific orders that we don't take scalps. We are the United States Cavalry, not a bunch of head-hunting cannibals. We're supposed to protect the whites and the Indians from each other out here. Even if we have to kill some of those Indians, we don't butcher their bodies."

The corporal dropped his hand to his side. The scalp hung limply in his hand, still trickling blood onto his blue pants.

"You got that, corporal?" the lieutenant said quietly as he

leaned across his saddle horn.

"Yes, sir."

"Okay, drop the scalp and let's move."

"Yes, sir," the corporal said softly and dropped the scalp. It hit the ground soundlessly, raising a small puff of dust into the breeze.

The lieutenant turned to the rest of his troops and said in a voice that was heard by each of the twenty men, "There'll be no souvenirs in this outfit as long as I'm leading it. We'll kill them when we have to, but we don't butcher them for a piece of hair to hang in the bunkhouse. Any man that disagrees gets a transfer as soon as we get to the fort. Any questions?"

A few horses shuffled nervously at the smell of fresh blood. There were no questions.

"All right," he said and turned back in his saddle. He raised his arm in military style and yelled, "Forward, ho-o-o-o-o."

They were off on a slow trot back to the fort. As Jeremy and Medicine Elk passed the grisly trophy now lying on the ground, Jeremy closed his eyes. Medicine Elk did not speak and Jeremy knew that he did not understand the English conversation. But Medicine Elk knew what had happened.

Jeremy was beginning to understand the gravity of the scalp. Taking Medicine Elk to the mountain was no longer as easy as he had originally assumed. They were now under the protection of the Cavalry. They would remain so until his sister Jennie was rescued or released by the Crow. The Crow would never release her now, Jeremy knew. She would have to be taken by force.

Silently, Jeremy wished that both of the Indians had been killed. He cursed himself for being so callous. At least if both them had been killed, the tribe would not have known for a few more days, maybe a week.

However, one brave had escaped. He would quickly return to the tribe and tell them the terrible news. That would cinch Jennie's fate. The Crow would not let this ignoble capture of Medicine Elk go without revenge. They would not overlook the killing of one of their honored braves.

They wouldn't keep Jennie long, Jeremy reasoned. It was too much trouble to watch her, feed her, and keep her from escaping. So long as they had her, the Cavalry would pursue them. They would soon pack their teepees and horses and head for new territory. There was safety in the Big Horn Mountains to the south and the rough Tongue River Breaks to the east. Either way, it would be impossible to find Jennie once they moved. She would vanish. She would either become a white slave girl or be killed. There were no other choices.

Jeremy shed quiet tears that afternoon in the saddle. He brushed his sleeve across his face so that the lieutenant and his troops would not see him cry. Medicine Elk saw the tears, though. He understood, too.

Medicine Elk was quiet that afternoon. Jeremy sensed that he was somehow changed. In the evening when they stopped to camp on a small stream, he did not continue with his death chants. There was a new stoicism in his face, a look of defiance and hatred. It scared Jeremy. If they were going to escape from the soldiers here or at the fort, he would have to have the full cooperation of Medicine Elk. Jeremy knew the old man did not trust him anymore.

The lieutenant ordered two men to guard Medicine Elk and Jeremy as soon as they camped. They were given a small fare of dry biscuits and beef jerky, the same food as the other soldiers were eating. A small cup of lukewarm coffee washed down the biscuits and trail dust. Medicine Elk refused the food. Jeremy knew he would.

Medicine Elk's legs were tied tightly with a light rope and his hands were tied firmly in front of him. The Indian was too old to put up much of a fight, the lieutenant reasoned, but he didn't want him to escape.

Jeremy was not tied, but was given very strict orders.

The lieutenant told him, "Until we get back to the fort and get this whole mess settled, you are staying with us. Any attempt to escape will result in the immediate death of this Indian friend of yours. There will be a number of bullets in your direction, too. These men are good shots and I'd hate to have to dig two graves in the morning before we move out. I like to get an early start."

Jeremy wasn't sure if the lieutenant was bluffing, but he was too tired and confused to test him. He curled up in a spare blanket given to him by one of the troopers, and within seconds, was asleep.

He woke up once and listened closely to the coyotes howling nearby. For a moment he was afraid that they were...no, they were coyotes.

SEVEN

They rode hard the next day, taking only a few minutes to rest and eat at noon. Jeremy relished the chance to get out of the saddle and stretch.

It was a treat for him since he wasn't used to riding. Jeremy's backside ached horribly. All he could think about was a soft bunk somewhere within four dry walls. A few gulps of water, a moment to close his eyes and they were in the saddles again. They pushed their horses northward. Shortly after dark, they rode into the fort.

He hadn't thought much about Jennie that day. His mind was numb from trying to stay in the saddle. He was too tired to worry. He knew, at least, that she was alive and safe. Did he say, safe? It was funny, he thought, but he knew these Indians were not intent on hurting Jennie. Just detaining her.

As they pulled up their horses inside the fort, the large wooden gate was closed and barred behind them. Two soldiers helped Medicine Elk dismount, and Jeremy slid limply to the ground. He had barely landed when the lieutenant was at his side.

"Come with me," he ordered as he strode past Jeremy.

"Where do I sleep tonight?" Jeremy asked.

"Shut up and follow me," the lieutenant replied as he headed into the darkness.

They walked across the compound to a small wood frame building. Over the door was a simple wooden sign that had been painted, "Colonel." Jeremy was ushered in and left to sit alone.

The room was sparsely furnished with only three chairs and a large well-worn desk. A yellowing map of the Montana Territory hung limply on the wall.

In a few moments, the colonel arrived. Jeremy could tell he had been roused from an early sleep because he was only partially dressed. The colonel was a large man with a long graying mustache that was well-groomed with shiny wax. His coat was loose, exposing his shirt and suspenders. The coarse hair on his chest poked over an unbuttoned shirt.

He walked around the boy once, then sat solidly in his chair.

"So you're the Higgins boy," he said.

"Yes, sir."

"Hmm, somehow I expected you to be bigger. They say you're seventeen."

"Yes, sir."

"Well, I hear that you've been chasing Indians out there since they killed your folks. My sympathies about your folks."

"Thanks."

"I hear you caught one, too. Good work. Was he one of the Indians that killed your folks?"

"No, sir. He's a Crow and it was Blackfeet that ambushed us."

The colonel looked to the lieutenant.

"It looks to me like we have to visit these Crow and get his sister back. We don't want them to harm her."

"No, sir," Jeremy jumped in. "You can't do that."

The colonel squinted and looked at Jeremy hard through the slits that his eyes made.

"Why not, boy?"

"Well, sir, I have a deal with the Crow. I take Medicine Elk, that's the old Indian, to the mountain. After he dies there, I go back to the tribe and they let Jennie go. You can't ride into their camp and take her like that. It's not part of the deal that I made with them. They'll kill her if you do that."

"You made a deal with them? You made a deal with the Crow?"

The colonel shook his head in amazement.

"You Easterners sure got a lot to learn about these Indians out here. Someday you will learn that Indians can't be trusted. They sent you off into the hills with some old man to get rid of both of you. They've already packed up and gone, son. If we don't find them right away, you will never see your sister again. Those Crow are not going to stay there just because they made some stupid deal with a white man, especially a greenhorn kid."

"They will stay there, sir. They told me they would stay there until I got back."

"And you believed them? Listen to me, son. You say that you trust them, right? Well, they don't trust you, do they?"

"Yes, they do. They gave me a knife and food when I left with the old man."

"Maybe so, but why did they send two braves to follow you to this mountain of yours? They didn't trust you to do it alone, did they?"

Jeremy choked. He couldn't answer. He knew the colonel was right.

"Lieutenant, I want thirty men saddled and ready for some hard riding at dawn. Pack the food in the saddle bags. Don't bring the mess wagon because we won't be gone that long. We've got to make a fast trip to save this boy's sister. I'll be leading the formation."

The colonel turned again to Jeremy. "Who is this Indian you captured? A chief or something?"

"No, not really. He's just an old man from the tribe and I didn't really capture him. We were just traveling together."

"Old man? Lieutenant, I thought you said that the Indian was a warrior?"

"Yes, Colonel. He's a little older than most of them but he could still kill any of us, sir."

The colonel smiled, "Maybe in your sleep, Lieutenant."

He addressed Jeremy again, "Well, son, let me ask you a couple more questions. If I understand the lieutenant right, you were traveling cross-country unarmed with a Crow warrior who doesn't speak English. Where were you going?"

"I'm not sure, sir. I think we were going to the mountain."

"What mountain?"

"I don't know. I was following him."

The colonel shook his head, "Where is your sister? Uh, what was her name?"

"Jennie, sir, and she is with the Crow."

"Oh, I see. So you captured this Indian and were hoping that we would find you and help you get her back. Right?"

"No, sir, I didn't capture him. I had to take him to the mountain."

"To the mountain? Why?"

"So he can die, sir."

The colonel shook his head.

"You're not making much sense, son. What about your sister? What happens to her while you are wandering around the countryside with this savage?"

"She is staying with the Crow."

"Of her own free will?"

"No, sir," Jeremy said softly.

"So she is being held against her will?"

Jeremy swallowed hard. He could see the trap that the colonel had laid for him.

"Yes, sir," he whispered.

The colonel pulled a map out of a desk drawer and stepped

toward Jeremy. He unfolded it and spread it out on the desk. He stabbed it with his pudgy finger.

"Son, this is the fort and this is where your wagon was burned. Lieutenant, show me where you found the boy."

The lieutenant eyed the map for a moment, then laid his index finger down.

"Right about here, colonel. In the hills between the Big Horn and Rock rivers."

The colonel studied the map for a few moments. "And you said that they were coming from the east?"

"Yes, sir."

The colonel took a deep breath and sighed.

"Well, my guess is that the Crow camp is somewhere in here," he said, outlining a small circle on the map. "Son, were those Crow camped on a small river?"

Jeremy looked at the map showing squiggly lines with names of rivers and mountains. The colonel was right. He evidently understood the Crow's movements. With his years of experience and his scouts' reports, he knew these nomadic people. Jeremy knew that the Crow were camped somewhere on that stretch of river. The colonel was pointing to the Crow and Jennie.

The colonel repeated his question, "Well, son, were they camped on a river?"

"No, sir. They were camped in some breaks behind a high ridge that had a lot of pine trees on it. There was a small hot spring there and a pond where they took baths."

The colonel looked down at the map and scratched his chin.

"Hmm, that's strange. It's probably one of the hot springs along this line of ridges. They usually don't camp on those springs this late in the year. It shouldn't take long to check them out, though. There's only three of them. Don't worry, son, we'll find your sister."

"When do we leave, sir?" Jeremy asked.

Thoughts of escape flooded his mind. If he had a horse and could get into the trees, he might outrun them.

"You're not going with us, son. This is a military matter now. We don't take civilians. Only soldiers and scouts. We can't risk civilian lives on a military expedition against hostiles."

"But I can be a scout, sir. I can show you where the Indians are camped."

The colonel put his hand on the boy's shoulders. "You are too young to be out there, son. You will stay here in the fort until we can rescue your sister. Then we'll get you back to Missouri where you belong."

Jeremy stamped his foot angrily. "But I *have* to go with you, sir. My sister is out there. You have to let me go."

"Sorry, son. I can't let you go."

The colonel turned to the lieutenant. "Take this boy to the visitors' quarters and post a guard at his door. He stays in the fort until we get back."

The lieutenant saluted smartly. "Yes, sir."

The colonel started to turn away but Jeremy grabbed his sleeve.

"Colonel, what about Medicine Elk, the Indian? What are you going to do with him?"

"He's in the stockade and will stay there until we return. Once we get back with the girl, he will be tried for murder and kidnapping." He paused. "And probably be hanged."

"But he didn't kill anyone or kidnap anyone, Colonel. It was the Blackfeet, remember?"

"We have no way of knowing that for sure, son. Besides, we've been having trouble lately with the Crow. This old Indian will be an example for the rest of them. They have to understand that the U. S. Cavalry means business. We can't put up with incidents like this against civilians. Someone has to be punished."

The colonel jerked away from Jeremy's grasp and moved behind his desk.

"But, Colonel, you can't do that. You can't hang an innocent man."

"I'm hanging an Indian."

"But, Colonel…"

"Dismissed," the colonel said in an loud, authoritative voice. "Take this boy to his quarters, Lieutenant."

The lieutenant grabbed Jeremy roughly by the arm and whisked him out of the room.

The colonel was left alone, quiet, standing at his desk. He looked at the map sprawled before him, thinking about tomorrow. It would be a hard ride and he hated to confront the Crow for any reason, especially something as delicate as this. He knew he had to find the Crow but didn't know what he would do when he got there.

Jeremy was quickly taken through the compound to his quarters, which were locked and a guard posted outside. The place was small, only one room in a wood frame building. It had one small window in the room that served as kitchen, living room and bedroom. It had a small table, two chairs, a small dresser, and a simple bunk. Dejected, Jeremy flopped down on his bunk.

In the twilight, he could see the hewn logs poking toward the moon. They offered safety to those inside but created resentment in those outside. He heard the soldiers scurrying about in the darkness, readying for tomorrow's ride. The hard heels of the sentry's boots echoed as they walked their posts on the elevated platforms. Occasionally, he heard a soldier shuffle across the wood porch and exchange a few words with his guard. The horses neighed softly to one another in the nearby stables.

Jeremy could not sleep. His mind was torn by thoughts of Medicine Elk. Jeremy had failed in his mission. Medicine Elk was probably sleeping on the dirt floor of the stockade, awaiting his execution. It was a sentence for crimes he did not commit. Worse, he would not even know why he was being hanged.

Jeremy lay on the bunk, trying to come up with a plan to rescue Medicine Elk. A tear formed in his eye as he thought about his friend swinging silently on the end of a rope. He knew he didn't stand a chance of getting Medicine Elk out of the fort alive. The guards were too alert and the pony soldiers would catch them in the open country even if they did get out of the fort.

He was afraid, too, that Medicine Elk's spirit was crushed. He was afraid that the Indian would resign himself to death. It was strange, he thought. His mission was to escort him to his death—and yet he had failed. Medicine Elk would die, yes, but not in the dignified way that he deserved. He would not die a warrior's death. To Jeremy, this was total failure.

Finally, he closed his wet eyes and slipped off to sleep.

Dawn brought bugles and reverie. The men were shouting orders and cursing the horses. The horses skittered around and neighed as they were loaded with saddlebags. Jeremy rose with a jerk and started for the door. Just as he stepped out, a blonde-haired soldier dressed in a bright blue uniform intercepted him. He barred Jeremy's path with his rifle.

"Where you going?" the soldier demanded.

"Uh, what's going on?" Jeremy countered.

"They're getting ready to go after your sister. They'll be leaving in about an hour, I guess."

Jeremy nodded.

The soldier said, "I'm supposed to take you over to the mess hall for breakfast. You're probably hungry since you got here after chow last night. You ready to eat?"

He realized that he hadn't eaten much since breakfast the day before. There had been some small rations at noon yesterday, but he had been too tired to eat last night. Jeremy agreed vaguely.

"Follow me," the soldier said and led the way to the mess hall. The food was good and quite hot. It was a wonderful change from the fare of the past few days. He hadn't eaten a good meal since they left the wagon train. There was pork—salty and tough but with plenty of flavor. There were eggs, too, and strong black coffee. He ate ravenously.

The young soldier stood guard over Jeremy's shoulder as he ate. After he finished breakfast, Jeremy turned to the soldier.

"I'd like to see Medicine Elk."

"Who?"

"The Indian that I came in with yesterday. Medicine Elk."

"We'll have to see the colonel first. I don't have the authority to let you see the Indian. I'll take you over to see the colonel."

Jeremy followed the soldier across the open courtyard to the colonel's office. The melee continued as the preparations neared completion. The horses were packed and tied to hitching posts outside the stables. The men were finishing breakfast and making final preparations. They scurried about the armory, the mess kitchen and the supply office.

The soldier knocked briskly on the colonel's door. The colonel yelled from inside and the soldier ushered Jeremy into the room. The room was still as sparsely furnished as the night before, but the colonel was fully dressed now. The long saber and sidearm strapped to his bright blue uniform commanded respect. The colonel stood proud and straight.

"Good morning, son. I'm glad to see you up so bright and shiny today."

"Thank you, sir."

The soldier said, "He wants to see the Indian, colonel. I told him that he would have to ask you."

"Yes, that's right, soldier. This is my fort. What do you want with that old Indian, son?"

Jeremy wasn't quite ready for the question.

"Uh, well, I wanted to see how he was doing today. He's an old man and we rode pretty hard yesterday."

"Come on, boy, don't give me that bull. You got more reason than that."

"Well, I guess I do, Colonel. I guess I feel that, well, I just don't want him to think that I abandoned him. We traveled together for quite a few days. I have a duty to him, I guess. He's became my friend and I want to make sure he's all right."

The colonel was silent for a moment.

"I guess I won't get a more honest answer than that. Not that I understand you. Corporal, let the boy see the Indian anytime he wants while we're gone. But keep an eye on him."

"Thanks, Colonel."

"You speak Crow, son?"

"No, sir."

"You want an interpreter then?"

"Uh, well, no. I think he'll be able to tell what I'm saying."

"Okay, whatever you want. But I still don't understand you, son. Corporal, if he needs an interpreter while we're gone, get him one of the Indian scouts. Dismissed."

The young soldier led Jeremy to the stockade. It was near the back of the fort away from the fort's only entrance. The stockade guard saluted the corporal and the corporal returned the salute.

"He wants to see the prisoner. The colonel okayed it."

"Yes, sir."

The guard propped his rifle against the wall. He picked a brass key from the large circular ring that hung from his belt. Cautiously, he unlocked the iron door and swung it open.

Jeremy looked into the dark musty interior. He could not see Medicine Elk but stepped inside the cell. Jeremy heard the guard swing the door closed and latch it behind him.

EIGHT

As his eyes became accustomed to the darkness, he could make out Medicine Elk's figure. He was squatting against the far wall, his arms laid across his knees. His head was rocking slowly from side to side. He did not look up until Jeremy spoke.

"I came to see how you were doing."

Medicine Elk's expression was blank. He did not understand the words that this young white man spoke. Jeremy softly approached him and squatted down. Their eyes focused on each other and Jeremy spoke again.

"I didn't want this to happen. I didn't want the soldiers to capture us. I wanted to take you to the mountain. It is still important to me that we go there."

Jeremy stopped for a moment.

"I wish you could understand me."

Although Medicine Elk did not understand the words, he somehow understood the concern. He sensed the sincerity from the heart and lips of this young white man. He was trying, Medicine Elk knew. Somehow, this white man would help him reach the mountain. This boy would not let him hang on the end of a soldier's rope. He knew that his body would not be buried in an unmarked dirt grave. Medicine Elk knew that his spirit would be raised to the sky for its final journey.

He looked deep into Jeremy's eyes and knew that his only hope was in this young man.

Medicine Elk slowly reached out his hand to Jeremy in a show of friendship. Jeremy was surprised at the gesture. Medicine Elk had understood his thoughts without understanding his words.

Hesitantly, Jeremy outstretched his own hand and took the Indian's hand. They had become more than friends in these last few days. To Jeremy, this Indian had become his own kin. There was joy in that realization.

Jeremy was saddened, though, as he thought about Medicine Elk's fate. In order to complete his mission, Medicine Elk would have to die. He knew, too, that he would once again become the enemy of the Crow. Their races would return to fear and suspicion of each other. These few days of trust between one white man and one Indian could not be sustained. In a critical time when it is imperative to men for their friendship to be strong and their bonds tight, it would be so. But soon, the bonds would fail and the friendship would vanish.

Jeremy held the old man's hand tightly.

"I'll be back soon," Jeremy said softly. "We will go to the mountain together."

With that, he released Medicine Elk's hand and stepped to the door.

"Guard, I'm ready to go."

Jeremy heard shuffling outside the door. There was a click and the door swung open. Jeremy stepped into the bright morning sunlight and squinted.

The organized melee in the fort's courtyard had nearly subsided. Only a handful of the men were not yet mounted. They had finished loading the packhorses and were inspecting the tack. They were careful because they did not want to enter Indian territory with faulty weapons or insufficient ammunition. They had to be ready if they expected to rescue the young Missouri girl.

Jeremy looked around quickly. The young blonde soldier who had escorted him to the stockade was gone.

"Where's the soldier that was with me?" he asked the guard.

"He'll be right back. Went to the latrine. You stay here where I can watch you. Guess he didn't expect you to be done so soon."

Jeremy nodded and looked toward the latrine. The door was closed and the soldier's rifle was propped against the wall. He took a couple of casual steps in that direction.

The guard stopped him, "Hey, you stay here where I can see you."

"I'm gonna wait by the latrine."

"You're supposed to stay here."

"Ah, come on. Let me wait for him by the latrine. Where can I go? You can still see me."

He turned away from the guard.

The guard shrugged and let Jeremy go. Like he said, where could he go?

As soon as Jeremy got to the latrine, he slipped behind the guardhouse. For a moment, he considered stealing the rifle. It would just be extra weight on his ride, though. The stockade guard might see him, too.

His heart pounded as he circled behind the guardhouse. He moved quickly behind the stable and toward the gate. The large cottonwood gate was open now, ready for the soldiers' departure. The horses were tethered to hitching posts, shifting nervously. They were saddled, bridled and each carried a saddlebag with food, canteen and bedroll.

Jeremy picked the horse that was nearest the gate and

tethered with three others. He quietly slipped up to it, quickly unwrapped the reins from the hitching post and turned the horse toward the gate. He swung himself into the saddle, slammed his heels into the horse's flanks and blazed through the open gate.

Above the pounding of the horse's hooves in the soft ground, Jeremy could hear the commotion behind him. Someone sounded the alarm as he raced into the open country on a cavalry horse. A bugle sounded and Jeremy heard men yelling at their mounts. Horses neighed loudly as spurs were viciously stabbed into their flanks. Soldiers yelled orders wildly. Their shouts faded with the distance until all he heard was his own horse's heavy breathing and hoofbeats.

Jeremy angled the horse to the southeast, toward the Crow camp. He looked over his shoulder and spotted two soldiers on his trail. They had beaten the others out of the fort and were spurring their horses on a dead run. He looked back again to see a dozen more soldiers strung out in ones and twos behind him.

He pressed his mount hard as they streaked across the sage-covered prairie. All of the horses were fresh, well-fed and well-exercised so Jeremy's pursuers were not able to close the distance between them.

Jeremy kept to the open country, hoping to string out the soldiers. That would keep them from getting organized for a while. He needed every second. He needed time to decide how he would evade them once he hit the streams and trees in the foothills. He knew that his only hope was to lose them in the maze of streams, rocky outcroppings and clumps of trees. He needed a place that would afford him and his horse temporary camouflage.

It took all of Jeremy's might to hang onto the horse as it raced fast and hard. Sure, he had spent weeks walking across these Great Plains to the Montana Territory, but he had never ridden a horse very often. He was a farm boy, not a cavalry soldier or Indian. He had raced plow horses in Missouri against the neighbor boy, but this cavalry horse was faster and leaner than anything he had ever ridden.

He prayed and held tight to the leather reins as they whipped against his thighs in the wind. He glanced over his shoulder again to see the two soldiers still there, solemnly dogging his trail. They were neither gaining nor falling farther behind.

After a half hour of hard riding, his stolen horse was starting to tire. As Jeremy entered the foothills with a few scattered trees, the terrain became rougher. Here and there were small outcrops of sandstone along the low ridges and large streams gushed freely through the grassy valleys. The country was still too open to try any evasive moves. Jeremy knew that he must soon take a chance—maybe only one chance—to trick the soldiers.

Most of the soldiers had fallen back to a single group by now to reorganize their strength and tactics. They were moving more deliberately at a fast trot, conserving their horses' strength and carefully following the easy trail left by the fleeing youth and the two closest pursuers. The two soldiers were unrelenting in their chase, however, and Jeremy continued to push his horse toward the heavy timber.

He reached a small stream that flowed gracefully through the willows and scattered cottonwoods in a long, low valley. The bottom was gravely and made for an easy crossing. Jeremy stopped in the middle of the ten-foot-wide stream and let his horse drink. He pulled the horse's head up after two gulps of the cold water, though. He didn't dare let the horse get waterlogged now.

Jeremy looked quickly upstream and downstream, trying to formulate a plan.

Suddenly, he heard the two soldiers behind him. He turned upstream and kicked his horse hard. The horse laid into the new task and sped up the stream. The hoofs generated a spray of icy water as they traveled swiftly around small bends in the treelined stream.

The two soldiers reached the stream crossing within a few seconds. They stopped momentarily and listened. One soldier studied the murkiness of the water.

"I think he went upstream, Jim."

"I ain't sure. I can't tell if he stayed in the stream or followed the trail over that ridge."

The second soldier nudged his horse to the opposite bank where he examined the sand along the edge of the water.

"He didn't come out, so he's gotta be upstream. Come on."

Both men stabbed their horses with their rounded steel spurs and moved upstream at an icy gallop.

Despite the noise of his own horse's hoofs on the gravel bottom, Jeremy could hear his pursuers moving behind him in the streambed. This simple trick would not elude them, Jeremy realized. These men had trailed horse thieves and Indians. They knew all the tricks. Jeremy would have to try again.

As he pressed his horse onward, he watched desperately for an opportunity. He needed help now and didn't know where to turn.

He called to his own god and prayed for guidance. There was a Crow phrase that he had heard Medicine Elk chant endlessly. Now it was engraved in his mind. He didn't know what it meant, but somehow it had given Medicine Elk a renewed strength when there was no way to continue. Quickly, he repeated it aloud. He said it again and a third time. As he rounded each bend in the stream, he would pray to his god and then to Medicine Elk's god.

He wiped the cold spray from his face and suddenly saw his opportunity. There was a fork in the stream where two smaller streams came together. Left or right, he thought, left or right. Without missing a stride, he turned left. He pulled his horse toward the smaller stream on the left and quickly disappeared into the brambles that crowded the banks of the stream.

Moments later, the two soldiers reached the fork in the stream.

"Which way?" the first soldier asked.

The second soldier shook his head as his horse sidestepped

the cold water rushing along its ankles.

"I don't have any idea. I can't tell a thing. Both streams are muddy."

"S'pose we oughta split up?"

"Guess that's our only choice. You take left, I'll take right. He don't have a gun, so don't kill 'im. If you see him, fire two shots. I'll do the same."

"Got it," the first soldier said as he spurred his horse up the left fork of the stream.

The stream was narrower, smaller and the brush grew thicker and closer to the water. In places, the heavy-leafed cottonwood branches hung over the stream. The soldier found he had to slow his horse so he could duck below branches and part them so that he could pass through. The trees were so thick that he couldn't see ahead of him. The branches, heavy with leaves, kept his vision to a few yards at most. He cursed the underbrush but steadily moved onward.

Jeremy was having the same trouble making his way through the brush, too, except that he was glad for the cover. He kept looking over his shoulder, hoping that he would not catch a glimpse of his pursuer. He was sure that the men had split at the fork, but he could not stop to listen for the sound of splashing.

As he traveled, he tried to formulate a new plan. It would be easier to outmaneuver a single rider than two. This thick brush was his ally, he knew, although it scratched and cut his face and hands as he swept it aside. His horse shied at the wild rosebushes because the sharp talons scratched its tender flanks.

As he rode upstream, Jeremy was afraid that the stream would divide again, leaving with him two very overgrown paths that would be too small to pass through. That would be a dead end, he feared. The only way out would be back into the path of his pursuer.

That was it. The only way out was the same way that he had come. That path was fastest, least painful, and would lead to freedom the quickest. Except for the rider that followed, it was the easiest way out of the deepening ravine that was climbing into the high hills. The mountains loomed above him periodically through an opening in the brush, feeding the streams with the last of the August snowmelt.

Jeremy slowed his pace fractionally. He watched closely for a spot where he could exit the streambed with little or no trace. He needed a place to hide for a few seconds until the soldier passed by. Then he could return to the stream and move downstream. From there he could find a better place to exit. He could escape the stream without any trace, then disappear into the eastern hills.

He moved more cautiously, more deliberately, analyzing each sandy embankment, each opening in the brush. Finally, he saw his opportunity. There was a small grassy knoll with plenty of heavy brush. The grass would not leave tracks like the sandy places. Quickly, he made his move. He had one chance and it was now.

He pulled his horse to a squatting stop, jerked the reins to the right and kicked his heels hard into the horse's flanks. The horse reared slightly, refusing to make the two-foot jump up to a grassy embankment.

Jeremy kicked again, this time harder. The horse paused and made the deliberate jump onto the grass. Jeremy quickly turned the horse hard to the right and took four steps into the brush downstream from where they had left the stream.

Jeremy slipped from the army saddle and reached for the horse's muzzle. He grabbed it firmly and held the horse's head close to his chest. He could not let the horse betray their presence.

Immediately, he heard the soldier tearing through the brush and galloping on the gravely stream bottom. The noise came closer until Jeremy glimpsed the bright blue uniform bobbing through the branches.

He feared for a moment that the soldier would see him too, but prayed that his dingy dungarees and wool shirt would hide him. He did not move, knowing that it would alert the soldier.

The soldier was upon him. In an instant, Jeremy could see

the young man's face, full of fatigue and blood from the rosebushes. Both man and horse were heaving heavily. They were drenched in hot sweat and icy water.

Jeremy closed his eyes momentarily and pulled the horse's muzzle tightly to his chest. The sounds crescendoed and—miraculously—began to dim. The branches muffled the breathing and splashing as the soldier's horse passed quickly in four long galloping strides.

Jeremy's world returned to quiet. A few birds complained upstream as the rider passed their way, disturbing their nests in the quiet summer hideaway. The rippling and gurgling of the water became the dominant sound and Jeremy breathed a heavy sigh of relief. He released the horse's mouth and stroked him on the brow.

"Good boy."

There was no time to relax, however. Jeremy knew that there would be another fork upstream. The soldier would hit the dead end and know that his prey had somehow tricked him. It would only be a couple minutes before the soldier would return along the same streambed, this time slower and more alert.

Jeremy quickly remounted. He nudged his horse and they gingerly stepped off the embankment into the stream. Jeremy turned downstream and laid his booted heels into the horse's flanks. In a moment, they were whisking downstream. Once he reached the fork in the stream where the two soldiers had split, Jeremy moved at a quicker pace.

Somewhere ahead of him were a dozen horse-soldiers moving fast to reinforce his two lone pursuers. Jeremy rode to the first grassy embankment on the east side and forced his horse up the small cutbank. They bulled their way through the thicket of chokecherries studded with willows, a few cottonwoods and periodic clusters of thorny rosebushes. They moved through the heavy vegetation that lined the stream for a hundred yards on each side.

Finally, they emerged into an open meadow where the withering grass grew belly-high on his gelding. It was easy traveling and the horse shook himself of the chill from the stream.

Jeremy moved higher into the foothills, staying close to the edge of the meadow. The heavy brush on the streambank was his cover. He did not dare ride the barren hillsides that rose to his left, since the soldiers would spot him against the sameness of the wheat grass.

He reached a small ravine that angled sharply to the east and crossed it, then moved along the ravine on the uphill side. He used the sparser vegetation of this ravine as a loose leafy wall between him and his pursuers.

He urged his horse onward, up the small divide between the drainages, until they rose out of the ravine. He moved low and fast across the divide and dropped into a new valley.

NINE

Jeremy kept to the trees as he traveled into the bright morning sun. The sun had been up less than an hour but Jeremy and his horse were already exhausted. They moved quickly for another hour or so, crossing two more small drainages before stopping to rest.

Jeremy slipped off the hard leather army saddle with a thud. Quietly, he lay on the ground. He held the reins in his hands, but his horse was too tired to move about. It was content to stand quietly for a few moments. Sweat caressed its sides and made ruts in the dirty lather on its shoulders and flanks. It pulled at a few shoots of drying grass, but didn't have the strength to chew it. The horse stood silently with the grass sticking oddly from the corners of his unmoving mouth.

The sky was deep blue above Jeremy. He lay on his back

and watched the small cirrus clouds move almost lazily across the vast expanse. The settlers were calling this the Big Sky Country and he knew why. When you stood on a hilltop or ridge in this new Montana Territory, you felt that you could see for a thousand miles.

It seemed there was always a mountain range in the distance in at least one direction, even as you crossed the rolling sagebrush and bunchgrass prairies. You could travel for days toward a mountain range and never get closer. This immense land was bounded by the most azure sky he had ever seen. The Missouri sky was dull blue by comparison, clouded by the dust blown from the thousands of acres of plowed ground. This country was so beautiful. So virginal.

And so deadly.

Jeremy sat up and looked around. A few birds in the nearby brush flitted about in the soft morning breeze. It was already warming up, promising to be another blazing August day in the Territory.

Nothing moved on the horizon. Jeremy figured that the soldiers were only temporarily baffled. Once they realized their mistake and were joined by the reinforcements, the soldiers would begin an orderly trek to the eastern hills. They knew where he was going.

Jeremy had an uneasy feeling that the colonel would lead his men toward the place on the map where he had laid his finger. He was not fooled by the fictitious mountain spring that Jeremy had described. This escape would destroy Jeremy's credibility.

The colonel would follow his own instincts now and lead his men to the long, low valley where he figured the Crow would be camped. And he would be right.

Jeremy thought momentarily about an attack on the Crow village. The soldiers might—might—stop long enough to negotiate with the Crow over Jennie. Jeremy was sure that the Crow would not give her up without getting Medicine Elk in return, though. But the colonel would never compromise. No trades. All or nothing. Give us the girl or we attack.

Jeremy knew that the Crow had no options. The colonel might decide to launch a surprise attack in hopes of finding the girl quickly. Besides, then he could kill as many Indians as he wanted.

With the recent attack on the Higgins wagon—even if it had been by the Blackfoot—there was enough provocation. The colonel was mad enough now not to bestow any mercy on the Crow. The Crow had the white girl, and that was enough reason for the U. S. Cavalry to intervene. It would be a bloody and one-sided battle.

Jeremy raised himself to his feet and stretched. His backside ached from the unforgiving Army saddle. His face and arms were scratched and bloody from the brush. He mounted his horse and again turned east. He pushed as hard as he dared without risking the collapse of his horse.

He rode until well after dark. As it grew dark, he found himself in the rolling hills that rose in the east. He doubted that the soldiers were trailing him anymore, but were following the colonel's uncanny senses. They would be traveling the trails and roads, moving at an easy canter or trot.

Jeremy knew he could travel faster alone than thirty cavalry soldiers could travel together. He would start earlier in the morning, stop less, and continue longer into the night. He had to beat them to the Crow village.

It wasn't until late afternoon that he realized his one miscalculation. The colonel knew exactly where he was going and how to get there. Jeremy's heart sank as he realized that he could be traveling miles out of his way on trails he did not know. He wasn't even sure of his destination, either in direction or distance.

Despair haunted him. He prayed again, bit his lip and moved on faster.

He stopped along a small creek when it had become too dark to see more than a few yards. A million pinpoints of sparkling lights lit the crystal night sky, but the moon had not yet risen.

Jeremy dismounted and uncinched the saddle from his

gelding. He tied the horse tightly to a low willow tree along the creek. From there, the horse could reach the water and the dry, matted grass along the banks.

As for himself, he found some dried meat in the army saddlebags and fell to tenderizing it with his teeth. It was salty, but the flavor was hearty and filling. Before he had finished his second piece of jerky, he slipped off asleep, crumpled against a willow tree.

The bright half-moon rose about an hour before dawn, illuminating the landscape with an eerie bluish light that created strange shadows in the trees and brush. Jeremy was awakened suddenly by a chorus of coyotes wailing of their plight.

He sat up with a start. He was groggy but rested, and his horse was standing quietly where he had tied him.

It was light enough to travel, he decided, and he needed the head start on the cavalry. He needed every extra minute and every extra mile that he could cover to beat the cavalry to the Crow village. He repacked the saddlebag, saddled the horse and stiffly mounted himself. With the nudge, they moved on again to the east.

About midmorning, Jeremy reached a small river, and sensed that this was the same river that the Crow were camped on. Downstream, the river's murky water poured into the mighty Yellowstone on its way to the Gulf of Mexico. Someday, this water would pass his old home in Missouri.

Somewhere upstream was his sister, the Crow village and danger. Behind him were over two dozen cavalry soldiers pursuing him and the Crow. The Crow, however, did not yet know they were now quarry of America's military.

Jeremy stopped for a few minutes to rest his horse. His own backside was taking a terrible beating from the saddle. He was not conditioned for so much riding. His thighs and butt muscles ached after only a single day in the saddle.

He did not relish the thought of another day in the saddle. But he had no choice. He hoisted his sore body into the stirrups once again and kicked the gelding in his flanks. They turned south toward the village.

It was just dusk when Jeremy reached the knoll overlooking the Crow camp. He kept to the side of the knoll so his silhouette on the horizon would not alert the Crow. He would need every advantage.

The cards were stacked against him already. The Crow scout who had escaped the assassination by the cavalry corporal would have returned to his tribe with the news. Medicine Elk and the young white man were captured by the bluecoats and headed northwest toward the house with high walls of wood.

The Indians could figure out the rest from there. The young white man would tell the bluecoats about his sister. Then the bluecoats would come to take her away. They probably figured that Medicine Elk was already dead now too, shot in the back by a bluecoat with an exploding stick.

As Jeremy sat astride his horse overlooking the camp, he realized that something was wrong. There was too much bustle in the camp for this time of night. The racks of dried meat had been pulled down and the horses were gathered together in a remuda to the south of camp. A few teepees had been dismantled, leaving the tall lean poles, skeletons rising mutely on the darkening plain below.

The Crow were breaking camp, ready for a journey. They already knew that they must get away, because the cavalry was sure to come soon. It would be slow going, though, because there were so many women, children, and old people. They would be gone by morning.

For an excruciating moment, Jeremy knew that riding into this Crow camp would be suicide. As soon as the Indians recognized him, they would pull him down from his horse and beat him. They would knife him because he had failed Medicine Elk.

His only chance would be to quickly find Crazy Bear, the only Crow that spoke enough English. Jeremy shivered. He didn't even know if Crazy Bear was still in camp. He could be hunting, scouting, or on sentry duty. He did know, however, that Jennie was somewhere in that camp.

He closed his eyes, took a deep breath and nudged his horse down the slope.

He reached the edge of the village without being seen. The Indians bustled about, gathering their goods. They were tying them onto travois that they would hitch to their horses at dawn. In the confusion, Jeremy moved quietly and smoothly into the camp.

He was well within the darkening camp when the cry went up. Women scurried for cover, screaming about a white man. In seconds, a dozen warriors brandishing lances and antiquated rifles appeared and closed in on Jeremy. He kept his hands tightly on the reins of his frightened horse. He made no fast moves.

Even in the fading light, it was easy to see that he was unarmed, being without a rifle, sidearm or knife. The braves circled him warily as he calmed his nervous horse. The women, children and a few old men gathered in a larger circle behind their men and the white intruder.

Jeremy held up both hands.

"I want to talk to Crazy Bear. Crazy Bear."

The Crow warriors looked quizzically at each other. They did not understand his white words and became more skittish. His horse fidgeted, stepping sideways and back again.

An old man moved inside the circle of men to get a closer look at the white man. He recognized Jeremy and said some words softly. Somehow, Jeremy knew that he had said, "It's the young white man that took Medicine Elk to the mountain."

Immediately, the braves began to yell and whoop. They jabbed their weapons at him. Jeremy's horse reared up. He pulled back hard on the reins, pulling the horse's head down. The horse reluctantly returned to all four feet. It backstepped away from the oncoming Crow braves until more Indians closed in behind it. It whinnied in fear.

Above the commotion, there came a shout. It came again and finally a third time. The braves stopped their deadly advance and stepped back. The rider and horse stood peacefully. Crazy Bear entered the circle and stepped up to Jeremy's leg.

"Fool," he said in a stern voice. "White fool."

"Crazy Bear," Jeremy said quickly. "I gotta talk to you. The cavalry, the bluecoats, are coming to kill you and take my sister. They will kill all of you, the women and children and the old ones, too. They want the girl and they will do anything to get her back."

Crazy Bear looked at Jeremy with a penetrating stare. "We know they come."

Jeremy breathed a bit.

"I see you're packing. That's good. You gotta leave tonight."

"We leave when the sun rises."

"They could be here by then. You gotta leave tonight."

"What you care if we die? We fight, we die. We are Crow. You go back to white soldiers. You not stay here."

"You have to listen, Crazy Bear. The bluecoats are close behind me. I've been riding for two days since I left the fort and they know where you are. You have to leave now."

"Why you come? You white man. We Crow."

Jeremy looked into Crazy Bear's eyes and said firmly, "I am Medicine Elk's friend."

Crazy Bear studied the boy for a moment. This boy had ridden into his enemy's own camp without so much as a knife. He had stood his ground against the warriors who provoked him. Even more, he had admitted that his heart was a brother to the Crow. He was a fool, yes, but his innocence betrayed only stupidity, not cleverness or trickery. Crazy Bear knew that this young white man was not capable of tricking them.

"Get off pony. Come with me."

Crazy Bear turned to one of the braves and yammered for a few moments, giving instructions. The man turned quickly and was gone.

When Jeremy slid from his army horse, no one made a move toward him. Each warrior stood his ground, his lance or rifle poised for an instant execution, but they did not move.

Jeremy gingerly slid past them and followed Crazy Bear to the center of the camp.

They entered a large teepee, the same one that they had held their council in a few days before. This was where Medicine Elk had told the council of his dream of the white man. Jeremy stepped to the rear of the teepee, around the small flickering fire, and squatted in the back. In a few moments, other Indians—the same group of elders he had met before—entered singly and in pairs. They squatted down next to Jeremy in a circle around the fire. The only ones he knew by name were Crazy Bear, Braids His Hair On Top and Otter, the Indian that had stopped the knife fight between Jeremy and another brave. In only two or three minutes, the circle was complete.

Crazy Bear, sitting opposite Jeremy, spoke first.

"It is by your bravery we let you talk. Tell us about bluecoats."

Jeremy swallowed hard and began speaking in slow easy sentences so Crazy Bear could translate his words into the Crow tongue.

"The bluecoats surprised Medicine Elk and me on the way to the mountain. They took us prisoner. They killed one of your scouts. I am sorry for that. The bluecoats took us to the fort over the mountains and put Medicine Elk in a....a very strong house where he cannot escape."

Jeremy looked around him. The elders were grim and agitated. They grumbled as he spoke. For a moment, Jeremy thought that the council was ended when Braids His Hair On Top stood up.

Quickly, he started again, "But I stole a horse and escaped from the bluecoats. I stole a horse from them and they chased me. I broke the white man law. Now they want me, too. Now I am their enemy."

When Crazy Bear finished translating, the council calmed down. Braids His Hair On Top sat down again. They looked askance at this young white man, curious of his motives but afraid of his intentions. They were afraid he had led the bluecoats to their camp. This meeting could be a white man's trick to keep them off guard. Braids His Hair On Top spoke a few words and Crazy Bear translated.

"He likes your courage. We Crow are great horsemen. We proud to steal horses from the white man."

Jeremy smiled and nodded. This was progress. He went on.

"The soldiers know where you are camped because you have been here for a long time. I told them you were camped at a hot spring in the mountains, but they did not believe me. They come on a different trail, but they will be here soon."

Crazy Bear translated, then added, "When the brave that followed you escaped the soldiers, he returned to us."

Crazy Bear pointed to Otter. Otter's arm was bandaged with a soft doeskin bandage where a soldier's bullet had pierced his flesh.

Jeremy's heart fell. The man who had saved his life had almost been killed by the cavalry. Jeremy sensed the anger in Otter's eyes.

"We argued for two suns about leaving this good place with water and trees and plenty grass. But we know we cannot stay. Women pack now. We leave when the sun rises tomorrow."

"The bluecoats could be here by then. You have to leave tonight."

"We travel by day. We do not move at night like the coyote or the mouse. We ride in the day like the bear!"

Jeremy took a long breath, "I saw the bluecoats at midday. They were near the place where this river empties into the bigger river." He bit his lip as he lied.

As soon as the translation was complete, there was a murmur and much hand waving among the members. His last words excited the council.

Crazy Bear spoke above the murmur, "One of the chiefs asks why do you tell us this? You are white like bluecoats. Bluecoats will try to take your sister from us. They fight for you, not us."

Jeremy paused for a long time as the murmuring died down, awaiting his answer.

"I am tired of seeing people die. All I want to do is take Medicine Elk to the mountain like his dream said, then take my sister Jennie back to the white cities. I do not want to see white soldiers or Indians killed. There has been enough death."

The translation took several seconds, and when Crazy Bear finished, it was quiet. Crazy Bear's own suspicion aroused one last question from Otter.

Crazy Bear translated Otter's question, "Which way to go? North, south, west, maybe east? Tell me."

Jeremy sensed that Otter was trying to trap him. Was he trying to get them to move into the path of the cavalry?

Jeremy shrugged.

"You know the land, I do not. You go any direction you want, but you must leave tonight."

Satisfied this was not a white man's trap, Crazy Bear held a conference with the elders. There were many minutes of arguing, bickering, and some of the older Crow warriors shot Jeremy menacing looks. Jeremy squatted quietly, awaiting his own fate and his sister's fate. He was unarmed and at the mercy of these powerful uncivilized nomads.

Finally, Crazy Bear announced the consensus, "We leave tonight. When the moon rises, we go to the hills."

Jeremy nodded.

He looked up and said, "What about my sister? I want her back."

Crazy Bear spoke to the other Indians gathered in the circle. Only Otter spoke and no one questioned his decision. Crazy Bear translated Otter's answer.

"No. You said you would take Medicine Elk to mountain. You did not. We keep your sister."

Jeremy nodded numbly, then rose.

"I want to leave now," he said.

"You are going to tell the bluecoats where we go?"

"No, I am going around them. I am going back to the fort

and take Medicine Elk away from the bluecoats."

"One white boy against the bluecoats?"

Crazy Bear shook his head.

"Big fool," he said flatly.

"Most of them are chasing you. There will be only a few at the fort."

"Wait," Crazy Bear said simply. He began another conference with the elders who still sat seated around the fire. The fire was low now and cast softening shadows on the interior of the sewn buffalo hides. They skittered this way and that, with no regularity, appearing and disappearing with the flickering flame.

"One Crow will go with you."

Jeremy shook his head. "No, I will do this alone."

"Otter will go. He followed you before. He saw his brother killed by bluecoats."

Jeremy winced.

Crazy Bear continued, "Otter show you faster trail to fort. He help take back Medicine Elk. Your journey is not complete. Otter's journey is not complete."

"I will travel alone."

"If you travel alone and take Medicine Elk to mountain, how will you find us? We leave this place. We go to hills and you will not find us again. Otter knows where we go. He bring you to us when your journey is complete."

Jeremy was silent now. He saw the wisdom of the Crow decision. Despite that, he did not relish the thought of traveling this country with a Crow warrior by his side, particularly one with a reason for vengeance. Crazy Bear was right, though. Jeremy would never find the Crow again once they disappeared into the rugged mountains and timbered breaks.

He nodded, accepting Crazy Bear's decision.

The council ended and the men rose to leave. Jeremy moved outside too, and stood alongside the council's teepee.

The word spread quickly through the camp and within a few minutes, more teepees were hurriedly torn down and folded onto the travois. Teenage boys brought the horses from the remuda and hitched the travois to their backs. In less than an hour, the Crow would move out and cross the river into the hardened land where the bluecoats could not find them. They would be sucked into the darkness.

Shortly, Crazy Bear returned to Jeremy, having given the necessary instructions to his own woman. It was dark now, and the only light in the camp came from the stars and numerous campfires. The moon would rise in a few more hours to give them the light they needed to escape.

"I want to see my sister before I go."

Crazy Bear stood for a few moments, as if he had not heard Jeremy's request.

"No," he finally said.

Jeremy did not lose his patience, but proceeded calmly to explain, "I just want to see her for a few minutes. If I do not see her before you leave for the mountains, she will worry about me. She will try to escape. She will return to this place to find me. If I can see her, I can tell her that everything is okay. I will tell her that I will find her again because Otter will go with me."

Crazy Bear considered Jeremy's arguments for a bit. He knew Jeremy was right. He did not need the frustration of having his white captive try to escape as they traveled in the hill country at night. This short visit might stop an attempted escape.

"You speak good words, young white man. Follow me."

He turned and walked through the hubbub of the camp. When they reached a teepee near the center of the camp, Crazy Bear called inside. A woman answered and Crazy Bear slipped through the hide door. Jeremy quickly bent over and followed.

He stood up in the firelight, nearly face to face with Jennie.

"Oh, Jeremy," she cried and threw herself into his arms. Tears welled up in her eyes and she hugged him tightly.

"God, I am so glad to see you. I thought that you would never come back to get me."

Jeremy firmly took her arms in his hands and held her at

arm's length. Her dress and petticoats had now been replaced by a more functional deerhide dress that fit her lithe body smoothly. There were small beaded decorations around her neck and her blonde hair was tied back in a greasy ponytail.

"I'm not taking you with me right now. I can't. Not yet."

"Jeremy, what are you saying? I have to go with you! These Indians are leaving here. They are running away from someone. It's got to be the cavalry. We have to get out of here and find the soldiers. If you leave me here, I'll never see you again. I don't know where we are going."

"Shut up and listen. I've only got a minute. The old Indian and I were captured by the cavalry before we got to the mountain. They took us to the fort and put Medicine Elk in the stockade. I stole a horse and escaped. The cavalry is moving in right now to kill these people and rescue you. But I'm afraid that you'll be killed in the fighting. Until I take Medicine Elk to the mountain according to my agreement with these people, they won't let me take you."

"But if we leave, how will you find us?"

Jeremy took a deep breath and gave Crazy Bear a quick look. Crazy Bear was getting impatient and would cut them short.

"I am taking a Crow warrior back to the fort. If I can get Medicine Elk out and up to the mountain, the warrior will show me how to get back to the tribe. He knows where you are going."

"But what if you…"

"Don't think about it, Jennie."

He quickly changed the subject.

"Are you okay? Are they treating you all right?"

Jennie held his hands tightly. "Yes, they haven't hurt me. They feed me whatever they eat themselves and I don't have to do anything. I belong to one of their chiefs, I think, because he comes to the tent sometimes at night. There are two other Indian women in the tent and I can hear him at night when he goes over to their robes. They giggle and make funny noises. Jeremy, I'm afraid."

Jeremy was somber. "Jennie, has he ever...?"

"No," she whispered, "he's never come over to my robes."

"Do you know what he does to the women?"

"Yes, and I'm afraid that he will come to my robes one night. Jeremy, what am I going to do?"

"I'll be back as soon as I can, but it'll probably be a week or so. I don't know. But I'll be back."

With that he broke away and dodged through the open hide door into the darkness.

"Jeremy, no!" he heard Jennie scream as he fled.

There was a choking sob, and Jeremy heard Crazy Bear issue orders to the woman in the teepee with Jennie. He knew that soon Jennie would be safe in the hills away from the oncoming cavalry. How ironic, he thought. She will be safer with the enemy than with the soldiers who were coming to rescue her. Why did he trust these Crow? He shook his head in confusion.

Outside the teepee, Jeremy stopped. Otter was standing at the door. His arm was bandaged with a cloth and leather thongs, covering the bullet wound from the encounter that cost him his brother. Otter held the reins of two horses, both sleek Indian ponies. Jeremy could see that they were well-suited to the hard traveling through brush and open plains. There were no saddles or tack on them, just a faded horse blanket and a rope halter.

Jeremy stood, frozen in his tracks at his new companion who offered him the reins of one of the ponies. Jeremy stepped forward and took it firmly. Quickly, he walked away from Jennie's teepee, leading his horse and Otter.

When the two men—enemies joined by a common duty to an old man—reached the edge of the dismantling village, they mounted their ponies. They walked over the river plain toward the low hills in the west.

The moon was just rising when they reached the top of the first knoll and looked back. The fires were disappearing now one by one, and the shuffling and conversing of the people was faltering in the wind. They could not hear any of the words, only the low murmur of the nomadic people.

Otter slipped from his horse's back and led his horse to a small clump of chokecherry bushes that clung to the slope. He motioned for Jeremy to join him. Jeremy did not understand but followed.

The two men squatted next to the bushes overlooking the river valley. When Jeremy pointed to the horses and then pointed west toward the fort, Otter shook his head. He gestured to himself, the fort and then to the east where the sun would rise in a couple hours. Jeremy did not fully understand the reason, but knew they would begin their journey when the sun had risen over the hills that would be hiding the Crow tribe. The moon had just peeked over the horizon and was bathing the slumbering land in soft blue light.

Jeremy and Otter watched the tribe begin its journey across the small river and up into the eastern hills. In groups of ten or twenty, the people and horses moved swiftly and noiselessly away from the camp. The fires were all out now, although a few still smoldered.

Jeremy saw something that he did not understand, though. After all the teepees were gone and the camp almost deserted, a dozen warriors rode out of the trees. Each man had the reins of three or four horses from the remuda, each with a pair of long poles strapped to their back. The Indians entered the deserted campsite and made wide circles around it with their ponies trailing them. They rode back and forth across all signs of the camp, then turned their horses south along the river. The dozen warriors disappeared into the grass and brush along the river and continued traveling to the south. Soon, they too were gone.

Jeremy stood up, ready to move as the sun started to peek over the eastern hills. Otter put his hand on Jeremy's arm and motioned him to sit again. Jeremy was impatient with this delay, but agreed to wait a few more minutes. Just as the sun was broaching the horizon, a cloud of dust appeared in the north and approached them along the river.

Jeremy realized quickly that it would be the colonel and

his troops. They had probably traveled most of the night once the moon gave them enough light to pick their way across the landscape.

When the troops reached the site of the camp, there was considerable yelling. The soldiers milled around and poked at the fires. A couple men dismounted and felt the rocks. Still hot. They can't be too far.

The colonel yelled orders at his men. There was confusion, a moment of indecision and the colonel pointed to the south. With a kick, the colonel's horse broke into a gallop, leading the formation in the direction of the dozen braves. The wrong direction. The trail of the poles in the ground was intended to look like the imprints of travois to an inexperienced tracker, and they did.

Jeremy thought, though, that it shouldn't have fooled an intelligent man like the colonel. There would be no moccasin prints mixed in with the travois trails and the pole tracks would be lightly imprinted in the soil because there was no weight on them. Jeremy figured that after the sun rose higher, the colonel would realize it, too. But for a while, the tribe was safe. They had a much-needed head start.

Otter smiled at Jeremy. Jeremy sighed and smiled back. The colonel had been fooled for now.

TEN

As soon as the troops disappeared to the south in pursuit of the dozen braves, Jeremy and Otter stood up. They mounted their ponies and headed toward the fort at a quick gallop.

Otter led them northwest instead of due north. When Jeremy left the fort, he had traveled east along the foothills to the Big Horn River, then south along the river to the camp. Otter's path, however, led them directly into the foothills. If they didn't get lost in the maze of ridges and coulees, the additional cover of the trees would help keep their advance secret.

Jeremy figured it would be slower going, though. The rough country would keep them from moving at more than a gallop. He did, however, know they wouldn't meet the Cavalry. They had a clear shot at the fort now.

Jeremy was wrong about the pace of their journey. The trails that Otter chose were narrow but clear. From a distance, the ravines looked choked with pine trees and Jeremy saw few paths. As they drew closer to each new stand of trees, though, an opening would miraculously appear. The trees parted before them and easy paths led through the ragged canyons. Otter knew the country like he knew the battle scars on his hands and chest. His years of hunting in these foothills would take them to the fort quickly.

They traveled quickly in the cooler pines. Shortly after the sun dropped behind the high mountains in the southwest, they came upon a small, clear-running stream flanked by a large open meadow. Night would be slow in coming because the mountains hid the sun so early in the evening. They moved across the meadow in the early dusk.

Shortly after the sun had fallen behind the mountains, Otter stopped his roan pony. He slid down and pulled the blanket-saddle from the horse. Jeremy followed. Otter hobbled the horses with lengths of rawhide and let them roam the meadow to graze and taste the cool stream water.

Jeremy built a small fire in a clump of willows a few yards from the creek. The willows would disperse the smoke so no one would suspect their presence. Otter disappeared for a while, leaving Jeremy alone in the meadow.

Jeremy was no longer frightened by the wilderness around him. He had spent the summer living with the land as he and his family had walked daily from Missouri. Even the last few days, he had survived off the sparse fare of the land. There were rabbits, sage hens, berries of all varieties and dried buffalo, courtesy of the Crow.

The land was nearly empty of other humans, though. A few prospectors dared confront the wilderness and fierce Indians for flakes of gold. In the higher remote mountains, the hardy beaver trappers crisscrossed the creeks in search of more productive waterways. Otter had pointed out beaver traps in the creeks that day, so Jeremy knew that the white man was already here.

At dark, Otter returned with three partridge that had fallen to his bow and arrows. Otter quickly cleaned the birds with his belt knife and plucked the feathers. He cut three long sticks and skewered the birds.

Wordlessly, he placed them over the small fire that Jeremy had built. In a few minutes, the juices rose from the birds and dripped hissing into the flames. The hot, fresh meat felt good in their stomachs, much better than the dried buffalo jerky that they had chewed all day.

Game was plentiful in the valley, and for a moment, Jeremy wished that he could stay here. The meadow was independent of the white men and Indians and their troubles with each other. This lost valley was so peaceful, so beautiful. He felt a pang of despair knowing they would leave here tomorrow and never return. He would never see the valley again. He knew he could never find it without Otter.

Shortly after dark, they let the fire burn itself out. They did not speak to one another that evening. The language barrier was insurmountable and Jeremy was still not sure he could trust Otter. Jeremy's journey with Medicine Elk had cost Otter a brother. Otter himself had been wounded.

Jeremy was comfortable during the day as they traveled, but to sleep in the darkness with this Indian nearby was unnerving. There was a reason for vengeance, Jeremy knew, and he was not sure of Otter's feelings about this mission. Had the elders chosen Otter for it or had he volunteered? Jeremy did not know.

Otter moved off away from the fire and found a place to bed down alone.

Jeremy curled up in a small grassy hollow against a pair of willows and pulled his shirt around him. He laid the horse blanket across his shoulders. There were no blankets tonight. Otter had packed the horses with only the bare essentials for this short trip.

It would be cool in the mountains tonight, but Jeremy decided it was for the best. The cool would keep him from sleeping deeply. He must stay partially alert in case Otter tried to overpower him in the dark. Jeremy did not have a knife anymore and he swallowed hard. He was ready to fight for his very life in an attack, though. He knew that those would be the stakes.

It was nearing dawn when Jeremy opened his eyes. He kept his head still and let his eyes search the meadow around him. The full moon was up and sunrise was only a few minutes away. A soft, dim light bathed the quiet landscape, belying the danger that made the hackles on Jeremy's neck quiver with fear.

He didn't know what woke him, but he felt a dangerous presence. Someone or something was moving slowly, cautiously in the brush to his right.

He watched intently for any movement that would betray the intruder's location. There were small sounds all around. An owl swooped through the trees and brushed its leaves. A field mouse scurried for cover. A wakening chickadee fluttered its wings and billowed its feathers against the morning cold.

There was another source of sounds, though, but Jeremy could not pinpoint it. Maybe the slight rustling in the bushes was a rabbit or a coyote. But no, it was as if he felt a hot breath on his neck that was not caused by the listless morning air. It might be Otter, but why would he sneak around in the brush?

The darkness faded into the soft, morning light. Jeremy watched the shadows changing slightly. He finally made out the form of a man. He was a large man, covered with fur and buffalo robes. He carried a long thick object, a club, no—a muzzleloader.

He moved with the stealth of a cougar stalking its prey. Jeremy heard the horses sidestepping behind him, made restless by the intruder. Suddenly, Jeremy realized that the man wanted the horses—and no witnesses.

Jeremy's mind raced. If he leaped to his feet to flee, the man would gun him down in an instant with a single shot. If the man crossed behind a tree or heavy brush, however, it might shield Jeremy's escape. If he lay still for a few more moments, he might have a chance.

Jeremy rustled slightly, poised for an instantaneous flight.

As Jeremy peered intently at the shadows, he saw the man stop his advance. There were a few long moments of silence and the man lifted the muzzleloader to his shoulder—slowly, carefully.

Jeremy knew he had been spotted. He had only a few more seconds to live. He must wait until the last possible moment. Petrified, he anticipated the next sound.

Then came the metallic click as the man eased the hammer back into firing position. At the last possible moment, he would leap to the left and roll into the bushes. On three, Jeremy thought to himself. He counted one, two...

Without warning, there was a thump. The man took a staggering step forward and dropped face forward into the brush. The rifle exploded with a thunderous fuming roar. Jeremy rolled away from his hollow and dropped behind a log. He covered his head and lay unmoving.

The quietness returned to the meadow. The man did not move anymore. Jeremy carefully lifted his head to look over the log. The crumpled shape of the furry man lay still in the grass.

Jeremy watched closely for any sign of life. The man did not move. Cautiously, Jeremy edged into the heavier timber. He suddenly realized that Otter stood fully erect beside him.

Otter was still holding a bow in his left hand, already strung with a second arrow. Jeremy slowly stood up beside Otter. They looked at the dead man. The thump that Jeremy had heard had been an arrow piercing the man's chest, killing him and saving Jeremy's life. This was the second time that Otter had saved his life.

Softly, Jeremy whispered, "Thanks."

Otter did not look at Jeremy but stepped to the dead body. He shoved the man over with his foot and grabbed the broken shaft of the arrow. He jerked it from the corpse and examined the arrowhead. He broke the shaft again, just above the arrowhead, and put it in a small leather sack on his belt. He would build a new arrow another day.

They left the body unburied in the brush. The magpies and bears would dispose of it. Jeremy and Otter had neither the time nor the tools for a good Christian burial. Besides, the mountain man didn't deserve a burial. Better he be eaten as carrion by the scavengers.

Jeremy closed his eyes and said a short prayer to God. This man would need His mercy during the Judgment.

Otter returned from ransacking the body and headed toward the picketed horses. It was morning; time to ride again.

Jeremy turned and joined Otter. They packed the buckskin saddlebags and laid the saddle blankets on the horses. In a few moments, they mounted and moved off quietly into the trees. They left the peaceful mountain meadow with only the smallest trace of their presence—the body of a white man. Even that would soon return to the earthen meadow floor.

They rode quickly again the second day. Shortly after noon, they approached the mountain pass east of the fort. They crossed the pass, keeping away from the well-traveled main trail. By midafternoon, they were winding their way down toward the fort. As the sun glowed brightly over the next faraway mountain range, a large open grassy plain around the fort opened up before them. In less than an hour, the sun would be gone.

Otter and Jeremy picketed their horses in the dense pine forested hillside to the south of the fort. Otter picked his way through the forest until he reached the semiopen valley floor. Here the stands of trees thinned to scattered clumps before giving way to lush grass. To the Indians, this was the Valley of the Flowers. To the white man, it was known as the Stillwater Valley.

Jeremy tried to stay close behind. Otter stopped as he reached the edge of the forest and waited for Jeremy to catch up. They both stood looking at the fort that lay serenely less than a mile away.

A score of teepees were scattered around the western edge of the fort. Small bands of Indians often sought protection from their blood enemies by camping around the fort. Also, Indians stopped here to trade with the white men.

The fort was more than a military base, it was also the hub of trading for the adjacent valleys. The general store housed inside the walls served as a gathering place for all the Montana races—Indians and white trappers alike.

A family could buy supplies to continue along the Bozeman Trail to Oregon at this supply store. Trappers came here to sell a few hard-to-find beaver pelts, even though they didn't fetch the fine price of only a few years ago. Mountain men and homesteaders bought ammunition for protection against the marauding bands of Indians and whites that haunted the plains to the east and the mountains to the west.

The wooden gate of the fort stood agape. Traders and Indians filtered in and out without regard to the soldiers. Indians were allowed inside the fort during the daylight hours, but were gathered up and escorted outside at dusk. Then, the gates were closed and secured for the night.

Otter looked at the sun as it hovered in the low western sky. In an hour, the mountains would consume it. They were running out of time. If they delayed more than a few minutes, the gate would be bolted against them for the night and their rescue attempt would be delayed until sunrise.

For a moment, Jeremy watched Otter's hard face. They both knew what must be done now, yet Jeremy felt the fear and tension inside this Crow brave. Otter would have to enter the very jaws of the enemy that was pursuing his people through the hills behind him. He had eluded them for months but now he was being asked, without words, to risk his hard-fought freedom for Medicine Elk, an aging relic.

Otter turned and looked square at Jeremy. Jeremy fathomed sadness and fear in Otter's eyes. He swallowed hard. They had no other choice. Fate was playing its hand.

Jeremy took a deep breath. He stood up and started a long easy lope toward the fort. He kept in the cover of the gullies, hoping that the movement would not attract undue attention from the guards on the towers. He could hear Otter behind him, moving easily through the grassy ravines.

His thoughts were racing. If any guard at the fort recognized him as the horse thief from a few days ago or as the friend of the old Indian, he would be arrested immediately. These soldiers had no sympathy for horse thieves that led the United States Cavalry on wild free-for-alls. He would just have to hope that the approaching dusk would allow him to slip in and out without being recognized.

As they reached the teepees near the fort, Jeremy and Otter slowed to a walk. The guards would be suspicious if they foolishly ran into the fort. They mingled in the lodges for a few moments, then advanced to the huge wooden gate. Once inside, they would have to make some quick decisions. For now, though, it was one problem at a time.

Jeremy and Otter walked quietly toward the gate, neither one daring to speak or look at each other. Their eyes were moving about quickly, desperately, searching for any sign of trouble.

"Hey, you," someone called above them.

They froze. They were caught. Should they run or stand and fight? For a fleeting moment, Jeremy verged on panic.

"Hey," the soldier above them called again. "You can't bring that Indian in here now. We're gonna close the gate in a couple minutes. Get him outta here. Now!"

Jeremy looked up at the soldier and waved. They turned back. He nudged Otter—who did not understand what was happening—and they stepped outside the gate. When they reached the outside wall, Jeremy crowded Otter up against the logs. With hand motions, he tried to tell Otter what had happened.

"You stay here, Otter. I will go inside alone. I will get Medicine Elk. I will be back soon. You stay right here."

He knew that Otter did not understand the words but hoped that he could read the situation. Otter crossed his arms and stepped into the lengthening shadows of the upright logs. Jeremy nodded to him and headed back into the fort.

No one paid any attention to Jeremy this time. It was

almost dark now, and the soldiers ignored the white people moving in and out of the wooden gate. Their only concern was the Indians. When an Indian approached the gate or was spotted inside the fort, their voices aroused. They would yell at the intruding Indian. If he failed to respond quickly, a nearby soldier would escort the offending Indian out of the fort. All part of the daily routine.

Tensions were high in the fort. Jeremy knew that he and his sister were the reason. The killing of Jeremy's folks had stirred the wrath of the local white citizens who felt their safety was again threatened. Innocent white people had been killed. The cavalry was simply acting in response. The cavalry was under pressure from the townspeople, ranchers and prospectors to bring the Indians to justice. They wanted revenge against the murderous savages who had done the killing. In truth, they didn't care who suffered the retaliation, as long as it was an Indian in the Montana Territory.

Jeremy kept to the shadows near the stables where he had stolen the horse only a few days before. He could not risk meeting any of the soldiers. At least a dozen of them would recognize him as the old Indian's companion. Quietly, he circled the stable and made his way to the stockade that confined Medicine Elk.

In the dusky light, Jeremy could see a bluecoat standing at ease near the stockade door. The soldier was young, probably eighteen or nineteen. The blue cavalry uniform hung loosely about the lad's shoulders and frame, deceivingly adding cushion and build to his lanky frame.

The young soldier was armed with a Springfield carbine, which was probably not even loaded. There was little risk of anyone attacking the stockade, so few of the guards ever bothered to load his rifle. The compacted powder in the capping breech-loader would only corrode the barrel and chamber. A loaded rifle meant a half-hour cleaning at the end of guard duty.

Jeremy watched for a couple of minutes, planning his moves. He tried to plan a release of Medicine Elk and their escape. Medicine Elk was too old to run. He was too frail to climb the parapets and drop to freedom on the other side. The old Indian was in too poor of shape for any such maneuver. It would be impossible—and suicidal.

After a few more moments, Jeremy made his move. With a catlike maneuver, Jeremy stepped up behind the young soldier and slammed his clenched fists onto the neck and shoulders of the soldier. The boy slumped to his knees, slowly loosening his grasp on his Springfield. Jeremy hit him again, harder this time. The soldier went down, stunned.

Quickly, Jeremy grabbed the soldier's collar and dragged him in the shadows against the building. The darkness was deepening quickly, hiding the incident from the guards that patrolled the parapets.

Jeremy fumbled through the soldier's pockets and found the large key ring. He unlocked the guardhouse door and pushed it aside. He pulled the soldier over the wooden threshold into the dark recesses. Jeremy pushed the door closed again without locking it. A passing soldier would not then notice a gaping door.

It took a few moments for Jeremy's eyes to grow accustomed to the murky blackness. At first, he wasn't sure that Medicine Elk was still there. He panicked. Maybe Medicine Elk had been moved. Maybe he had already died.

But softly from the far corner came the familiar whispering chant that he had heard during the nights on the open prairie. The sing-song lament revealed the weariness of the old Indian. Sometimes, even the whisper was lost for a few phrases. Then Medicine Elk would lay his head back and sing the words clearly again.

Swiftly, Jeremy unfolded his new scheme. He stripped the blue uniform from the young soldier and unclothed himself. He slipped on the cavalry pants, shirt, jacket, boots and belt. He stood up and brushed the dirt from the blue uniform. Jeremy grabbed the soldier's hat as the final touch. The uniform fit Jeremy better than it had fit its original owner, although the boots were a size too small. It would do, Jeremy decided. It would have to do for now.

Jeremy stepped quietly to Medicine Elk's side and held down his hand. The old man looked up at the soldier, noticing him for the first time. He grumbled and crouched farther into the dark corner.

"Medicine Elk, it is me. It's Jeremy. I have come to take you to the mountain like you dreamed."

The old man did not respond to Jeremy's voice. The blue uniform was saying all the words that Medicine Elk cared to hear. He would not listen to the bluecoat. He would never listen again. He would sit and chant until he passed through the hole in the sky.

Jeremy knew that he was wasting time. The young soldier might regain consciousness and sound the alarm. That would put a permanent end to the rescue. Knowing that, Jeremy moved with little sympathy.

Jeremy grabbed Medicine Elk by the arm and jerked him to his feet. If Medicine Elk thought of him as a bluecoat, Jeremy would treat him like the bluecoats.

Jeremy pushed him toward the door, but Medicine Elk feebly recoiled. It was safe and dark in this place. The outside world was filled with soldiers and white men with hate and rifles. Jeremy pushed him again and Medicine Elk stumbled over the threshold into the waning light.

Jeremy closed the guardhouse door and locked it this time. He threw the keys back into the guardhouse where they would lie hidden in the darkness until the guard came to. Jeremy grabbed the Springfield from the dust and jabbed it at Medicine Elk. Medicine Elk understood the white man's gun. He shuffled quietly wherever the soldier guided him.

Jeremy steered Medicine Elk across the main grounds toward the gate, staying in plain sight of the guards. It was almost dark now and the guards were latching the gate for the night.

"Hold it," Jeremy hollered at one of the soldiers. "I found this Injun over by the stables. Let me run him outta here."

The guards obediently unlatched the gate and swung open

one of the wooden doors. As Jeremy pushed Medicine Elk outside, he realized that the guards expected him to stop at the gate.

Angrily, he announced to the guard, "I'm gonna take this Indian down to the coulee and remind him that he's not supposed to be in the fort after dark. I'll be back in a coupla minutes."

"Don't let the colonel find out," one of the guards chuckled as he closed the gate behind him. "He don't cotton to us beatin' 'em up too bad."

"Don't worry about me," Jeremy said confidently. As the gate latched behind him, he sighed heavily.

ELEVEN

Otter leaped at Jeremy from the dead-black shadows. His knife was raised high, poised for killing the bluecoat.

Instinctively, Jeremy swung the Springfield up hard against the Indian's arm, sending the knife skittering in the dirt. Jeremy jumped back and leveled the rifle at his attacker.

"Otter," he hissed. "Hold it. It's me, Jeremy. Take it easy."

Bewildered, Otter stopped. He squinted in the darkness, trying to unravel the confusion. It was the uniform of his enemy, but the voice of his friend.

When he recognized Jeremy, he smiled. He understood Jeremy's plan. In that moment, he realized too the immense risk that Jeremy had taken to rescue Medicine Elk. This young white man, now dressed in the treacherous blue uniform of his people's enemy, had risked his own freedom and life for this old man, a part of Otter's own tribal family.

Jeremy lowered the rifle barrel, pointing it harmlessly at the dirt. Otter quietly stepped within arm's reach of Jeremy. He stretched out his arms and put his hands on Jeremy's shoulders. He clasped tight. It was his only way of saying thanks.

At that moment, a cry went up inside the fort. The stockade guard had regained consciousness and roused a passing sentry. There was confusion and yelling in the compound. Jeremy and Otter heard men running about wildly, yelling orders and cursing.

Jeremy flung the unloaded rifle into the dirt and grabbed Medicine Elk by the arm.

"Come on," he said, "we've gotta get going, quickly."

He pulled Medicine Elk along, knowing that he had not understood what had happened. Medicine Elk hesitated, confused by the soldier who had taken him from the guardhouse. He did not understand why the bluecoat was leading him away from the fort.

Otter quickly intervened, saying a few words in Crow to the old man. Otter said the words again and they both looked at Jeremy.

Medicine Elk stepped up to Jeremy as Jeremy removed his cavalry hat. Medicine Elk's eyes widened slightly and he muttered something to Otter. Otter nodded, wordless. Medicine Elk looked around quickly, then strode briskly into the coulee. The darkness enveloped him. Jeremy disappeared closely behind him.

Jeremy looked behind him to see that Otter had not followed them. Otter grabbed up the Springfield and sprinted toward the nearby teepees where a small group of braves had gathered near a fire. They were listening to the confusion inside the fort.

Jeremy cursed under his breath. What was he doing now? I need him, he thought.

Jeremy didn't have time to stop and didn't dare yell to him. Disgusted, Jeremy led Medicine Elk rapidly up the coulee toward the two horses that he and Otter had tethered in the trees. It would be hard to find them in the dark, but the horses were their only salvation. Medicine Elk found new strength in his release, and he stayed very close behind Jeremy.

Suddenly, they heard a horse thundering up the coulee behind them. It was coming straight at them, closing rapidly. They heard the horse bellow, its legs and sides brushing the tall grass and wild rosebushes. The hooves slammed heavily on the gravel bottom of the coulee.

Jeremy frantically looked around and leaped for cover under a wild rosebush. As he rolled onto his stomach and looked back, he realized that Medicine Elk had not followed him. Medicine Elk was still standing on the trail, in plain view of the oncoming rider. The horse was going to trample him.

"Get down, you fool," he cried. "They'll see you. Get down."

The old Indian stood his ground as the horse galloped closer. The horse and rider exploded from the brushy coulee and suddenly swerved to miss the old man who stood quietly in the darkness. The rider expertly jerked the horse back on its haunches, spewing dirt onto the old man's leggings.

Jeremy looked up to see Otter slide off a small pinto horse. Otter grabbed the old man by the hands and spoke to him in quick, desperate tones.

Jeremy now realized why Otter had not followed them. He wanted the unloaded rifle for trading, not for defense. He had bartered with the small group of braves outside the fort, trading the cavalry rifle for a pony. The Springfield was a great fighting advantage. Even though it was illegal for an Indian to own one, most braves would take the risk.

For that trade, Otter had secured a fresh horse for Medicine Elk. Now they could all three travel on horseback.

Jeremy stood up and brushed the dirt from his blue trousers.

"How did you know it was Otter?" he angrily asked Medicine Elk. "It could have been a soldier!"

As if Medicine Elk understood Jeremy's question, he went

over to the pony and lifted a front leg. He pointed to the unshod hoof. No horseshoes, Jeremy realized. Medicine Elk could tell that the rider was on an unshod horse, so it was obviously not cavalry. Jeremy nodded. He was a wise man.

Otter hoisted Medicine Elk onto the pony and handed the braided leather reins to the old man. Otter signaled to Jeremy and they moved off at a trot, followed closely by the pony and rider. They headed to the trees where they had tethered their horses.

There was less commotion behind them now at the fort. The troops were organizing themselves now that the initial panic had subsided. The lieutenant had sorted out the facts from the excited young sentries and the embarrassed guard. Seething with anger, he readied plans for an immediate pursuit. If the colonel found out the old Indian had escaped, he would be court-martialed.

He quickly assembled a detachment of soldiers. The men scurried around, saddling and bridling the horses. The lieutenant ordered the men to head out the moment they were mounted.

Within moments, they started to leave the fort in groups of three and four. Their instructions were to spread out and pick up the trail. If they spotted the escaped Indian, they would fire three pistol shots.

Jeremy and Otter made their way through the coulee as it rose toward the mountains and pine-covered foothills. Medicine Elk stayed on their heels, not knowing their destination or route.

Jeremy looked back to be sure the old man could stay on the galloping horse. The old man looked strong again, stronger than he had ever seen him. His face was bright and smiling as the moon rose over the eastern hills, illuminating the chase. His heart was soaring. He was free again. The wind whipped through his long hair and the brush tore harshly at his buckskins.

Jeremy smiled to himself, too. He and this aged Indian brave who was nigh to death had confounded and defeated the

United States Cavalry. It was an insignificant victory, but there was glory, nonetheless.

Despite the small conquest, they were now racing for their lives. Each one wanted to keep and savor that victory at sunrise.

They reached the horses, quickly untied them and swung onto the bare backs. All three riders dug their heels into their fresh mounts and turned toward the east. Otter led the small group into the pine forest. He knew it well, even in the faint moonlight.

The rhythm of a running horse between his legs imparted new strength to the old man. Medicine Elk lay low on his pony, trying to absorb the pounding beneath him.

Jeremy wondered if Medicine Elk would last the night and the hard ride that lay before them. At least this way, he thought with a sad heart, Medicine Elk could die on the back of a strong pinto horse. With the cavalry chasing them, it would be a warrior's death. Silently, they sped through the moonlight toward the Crow country.

Jeremy clung tightly to his horse's mane. There was no saddle or blanket to cushion the impact or support his legs. The backbone of his horse bruised his buttocks with every long stride.

The hammering kept his brain from forming clear thoughts. He tried to envision the next few days, worrying about Jennie and Medicine Elk. All he could see was the fleeting shadows of the two Indian horsemen that raced pell-mell ahead of him in the trees. All he could hear was the bluecoated pursuers bent on capturing them or taking their corpses back to the fort.

The lieutenant did not like being fooled. Behind him, he could sense the anger.

On and on they rode into the endless sea of trees and darkness.

Jeremy realized he must have fallen asleep in the saddle only when he awoke in the morning. He was still astride his mount, bobbing softly across a grassy hillside. He caught himself as he almost fell off his horse.

Startled, he shook his head. Otter and Medicine Elk were ahead of him a few yards. Otter was dozing slightly while Medicine Elk was draped across his pinto's neck.

Otter roused himself enough to change direction, drifting down the brush-covered coulee bottom. They stopped at a small creek hidden by a heavy growth of chokecherries. Otter slipped soundlessly from his horse. He moved back to Medicine Elk and lowered the sleeping old man to the grassy floor.

Jeremy slumped off his horse, too, and Otter tethered the three together near the water. All three men were soon unconscious in the heavy deep grass, unaware of the crystal white cirrus clouds that raced eastward across the blue Montana Territory sky.

Jeremy woke suddenly as Otter shook him roughly. He squinted into the bright midmorning sun and shook the cobwebs from his mind.

Otter whispered loudly and pointed frantically to a ridgeline on the distant horizon. Jeremy looked and saw nothing, then shrugged his shoulders at Otter. Otter grabbed the sleeve of Jeremy's blue uniform and rubbed the cloth with his other hand. He pointed in the distance, then rubbed the cloth again.

This time Jeremy saw it. A light cloud of dust rose calmly from around the far bend in the coulee. It neared the bend until the cloud was less than a quarter-mile away. Riders in blue uniforms appeared out of the dusty fog, pacing their horses in an animal-saving canter.

Jeremy sprang to his feet and the two of them snatched Medicine Elk from his nap. Medicine Elk staggered under the veil of sleep. He cursed Otter as they hoisted Medicine Elk onto the back of the pinto. Uncooperative, Medicine Elk voiced another scathing remark at Otter.

Otter stepped back from Medicine Elk's horse and pointed at the approaching cloud of dust and its riders. Medicine Elk's eyes widened slightly. He looked back quickly at Otter. Otter spoke quietly and Medicine Elk nodded.

Medicine Elk jabbed his moccasins into the flanks of the pinto and eased the horse into a slow run. Otter took two quick steps to the remaining pair of horses and mounted one of them. Jeremy scurried to grab the reins of his own horse and leaped onto its back. He stabbed his boots hard into his horse's sides, urging it on. They were rested now, but they had lost too much time.

Jeremy looked behind them as they fled out of the coulee. Otter angled them toward a line of ridges to the east. The cavalry horses were also running, pursuing the three small clouds of dust that passed silently and effortlessly over the open hillsides.

After an hour of hard riding, the cavalry seemed to be lagging. Jeremy realized finally that the lieutenant had probably traveled all night at a slower pace, hoping to catch the escapees. The three-hour rest among the shady and wet creek bottom was proving to be a slight advantage for Jeremy and the two Indians. It was only the renewed freshness of their horses that was saving their lives this time.

Jeremy expected them to continue east, heading for the small river where the Crow had camped. He guessed that Otter would pick up the trail of the moving lodges and follow it to the new camp—and Jennie.

They didn't push their horses quite as hard now that the cavalry was falling behind. They would save their horses' strength for a final run that might be required later. Even though the cavalry had fallen back to over a half-mile, Jeremy was sure that a confrontation was inevitable.

The sun had risen to its full height, baking down on the men as they steadily and quickly traversed the grass and sagebrush country. The August sun was relentless in the Montana Territory. Coupled with the dry winds from the south, the bunchgrass was brittle. With every step, the dust erupted from the grass and attached to the sweating flanks of their horses.

Jeremy felt the sweat roll down his spine and wiped it from his forehead. They needed to stop for water again soon. The horses wouldn't last much longer without it.

Suddenly, Jeremy realized that the sun was striking him full on the back. That meant they weren't traveling east, but due north. He pulled his horse up to a halt and yelled at the figures ahead of him. Otter slowed his own horse and turned back to Jeremy. Jeremy pointed to the sun, then pointed east toward the Crow's old camp. He turned his horse east and nudged a couple of steps.

Otter quickly trotted his horse up to Jeremy. He sat straight up, full on the back of the heaving horse. Otter pointed east and shook his head. Then he pointed north and pointed to Jeremy and himself. Jeremy shook his head violently and forced his horse to take a few more steps to the east.

Otter shook his head again and made a wide circle with his arm. In finality, he pointed to the dust cloud that rose silently behind them. The soldiers.

Jeremy stopped. He understood now. They were taking the soldiers away from the camp. They would double back later, going east and south to rejoin their people. For now, though, they must lead the soldiers away from the tribe. When the tribe was moving, it was most vulnerable. Otter and Jeremy must protect the Crow.

Otter turned back to the north and Jeremy fell in behind him. They traveled until dusk without further words. The soldiers stayed on their trail, lagging farther behind as the afternoon wore on.

Shortly before dusk, the three riders stopped. Jeremy looked on the horizon behind them but could not discern the dust cloud that had dogged them all day. The cavalry was at least two or three miles behind them. Soon, they would surrender the chase and return to the fort. Trying to catch Indians in this country was a difficult task, even for the lieutenant and his seasoned troops.

The three men watered their horses at a small spring that flowed lazily from the bottom of a brush-covered coulee. Jeremy lay on the edge of a grassy bank and washed his face. The cool water refreshed him and gave him renewed vigor. They rested in the sparse shade for only a few minutes. With a new determination, they remounted their ponies.

Otter led the small troop out of the series of winding coulees and turned away from the setting sun. They were traveling east now, and would soon intersect the trail to the Crow's old campsite. Probably tomorrow, they would reach the river and ford it. Then they would follow the river until they found the trail. The tracks of the lodgepoles dragged by the horses would be easy for Otter to find.

They traveled until long after dark, stopping finally in a small dried-up streambed. There were sandstone cliffs jutting into the moonlight on one side of the gravely streambed. Otter pointed to the cliffs and Jeremy nodded. He and Medicine Elk followed his lead.

They picketed the horses on the greasy juniper that clung tenaciously to the cliffs, then laid themselves down in the warm soft sand. Otter passed out one pancake-sized piece of buffalo jerky to each man. Along with the jerky, each man took a long sip of tepid water from Otter's water skins. Jeremy ate only half of his jerky before slipping softly into an exhausted sleep.

Otter was moving about camp shortly before sunup. Jeremy didn't open his eyes to see him, but sensed the Indian's movements. The long ride had sapped his physical endurance. He was slow to wake. His eyes were closed as his mind passed through the clouds of sleep.

Jeremy thought how strange it was that he felt safe with these two Indians. His parents had so recently been viciously murdered by the Blackfoot. Now these Crow were holding his sister captive somewhere in the rough pine hills of southeastern Montana Territory. His own white people were fighting an undeclared war with them, even now pursuing him as a horse thief and accomplice.

He remembered the Missouri newspapers that told of the brutal killings on the isolated settlers and travelers in the Great American Desert. He had seen that up close. Now he had no gun and no knife to defend himself.

And yet he lay here with two of them in the heart of their own country, risking his life with theirs for a reason he wasn't sure he even understood. Somehow, he felt safe. He slipped back into sleep.

As the night gave way to the advancing daylight, Otter shook Jeremy. Jeremy's eyes opened slightly and Otter pointed toward the rising eastern sun. It was still hidden behind the low hills, but Jeremy nodded. The trail was not yet ended.

His body was racked by the days of running and riding. For a moment, he considered telling Otter to leave him. He was too tired to go on. Otter and Medicine Elk could return to the Crow. Jeremy would somehow make his peace with the soldiers when they finally caught him. He knew he couldn't quit, though. Jennie's life depended on him. He couldn't let her down.

Otter shook him again, harder this time. Medicine Elk moved about as the traces of early morning fog clung in scattered pockets in the coulee. Medicine Elk was hunched over from both cold and age.

Jeremy gathered his feet under him and tried to stand. His legs were numb from yesterday's ride. The constant pounding of his horse caused his thighs to ache. Jeremy staggered for a second, then recovered himself. He picked up the uneaten buffalo jerky from the night before and stuck it in his shirt pocket. He would eat it as they traveled.

They did not travel as fast that next morning. Jeremy knew that Otter was allowing both him and Medicine Elk to relax slightly as their horses walked easily toward the rising sun. The rhythm of his horse and the cool morning air was punctuated by trills of the black and yellow chested meadowlark. Gradually, they lulled Jeremy back into sleep. He laid his head on the horse's mane and dozed again.

It was midmorning when Jeremy came to again. The slow rocking of the horse had kept him asleep for a couple of hours. Jeremy twisted his head around, trying to snap the aches out of his neck. He shook his hair and ran his fingers through it. The matted clumps were full of grass and leaves. He stretched his arms and looked around.

Otter and Medicine Elk plodded on a few yards ahead of him. Medicine Elk was dozing, his head flopped down onto his chest, but Otter sat up straight on his pony. He looked far into the distance, searching the horizon. His eyes were alert for clues to the location of the soldiers and of his own people.

Jeremy realized that they were now traveling east toward the river and the Crow band. They had switched from their northerly direction—a zigzag tactic to confuse the cavalry. They were now on the home stretch toward the rugged hills beyond the river.

By evening, they would reach the river where they would pick up the trail of the lodgepoles. The deep scratch marks in the earth would be easy to find and easier to follow.

Jeremy turned in his saddle and looked at the horizon behind him. He expected to see a small dust cloud in some distant coulee, rising from the soldiers' horses.

There was no dust cloud. He searched the horizon carefully, but could not find anything that would betray the cavalry's presence. The lieutenant must have turned back to the fort or somehow lost their trail. Whatever happened, the soldiers were no longer following them.

Otter saw Jeremy scan the horizon. When Jeremy looked back at Otter, Otter shook his head and shrugged his shoulders. He did not know what happened to the pony soldiers, either. At this point, he didn't care. As long as they reached the tribe safely, the bluecoats did not matter.

The sun baked them again in the afternoon. They rode slowly, unhurried by the summer sun or their mission. The cavalry had turned back, relieving the pressure on the three men. The Crow were on the move now, but Otter knew the country and he knew his people. He could find them even without following the trail of the travois.

The riders stopped whenever they crossed a sluggish tepid waterhole. The chokecherries and buffaloberries often nestled small watering holes at the bottom of the swales in the open prairie.

Otter knew that Medicine Elk's strength was failing so they rested frequently. His vitality was gone now. Both Otter and Jeremy knew that he might not make it back to the tribe alive. At least he would die in the saddle, though. Such was a better death than hanging on a white man's rope or dying in a cold dark prison.

They must get into the foothills, though. They could find a tree there. Medicine Elk could find his final rest there. The Crow would not bury a warrior in a damp hole in the earth. Nor would they leave the body for the coyotes to tear apart and scatter the bones.

The soul must be given a head start to the land beyond by raising it onto a platform or placing it in the crook of a tree. Only there could the body and soul be at peace.

TWELVE

Jeremy watched the sky closely that afternoon. He dreaded the thunderstorms that were building on the western slopes of the mountains.

The billowy cumulus clouds sailed innocently overhead, growing ominously as they drifted. He didn't mind the deafening roars of thunder and blinding flashes of lightning, but he hated the drenching rains. It seemed to him that the storms on these northern plains were worse than in his home state of Missouri. The tempests were fiercer, more violent, more variable.

By late afternoon, the three riders topped a small ridge. They looked out onto the empty river valley where the Crow had camped until a few days ago. Medicine Elk perked up slightly as Otter pointed to the campsite, saying a few words to the old man. There was a new spark in Medicine Elk's eyes.

Jeremy figured that they would catch up to the tribe in a day or so. A band of Crow could not move near as fast as the three unburdened men on horseback. By tomorrow night, they would overtake them—and his sister Jennie. He pressed his horse onward.

The three horsemen descended into the broad river plain. They crossed the open meadow dotted with teepee rings and blackened rocks. There was little evidence of where campfires had warmed the evenings and cooked the buffalo and deer meat. Jeremy saw few traces of the Crows' stay.

By next spring, the grass would recover where the horses had grazed. The teepee rings and firepits would be hidden by new green growth. Then someday, the Crow would camp here again.

They crossed the Little Big Horn River at a ford a hundred yards downstream from the old campsite and picked up the lodgepole trail beyond a ridge to the south.

The long wooden poles that dragged in the ground behind the horses had scratched furrows in the soft soil. That made tracking the fifty-odd travois with horses, women, children and warriors an easy task. The trail climbed into the rolling hills to the east of the river where Jeremy could see mountains in the far purple distance.

Medicine Elk's strength began to deteriorate as soon as they passed the old Crow campsite. Jeremy watched the old man struggle to keep his balance and keep up the slow pace set by Otter.

Medicine Elk wound his hands tightly in his mare's mane to keep himself from falling off. The old man was determined, but his frail body was unable to stay up with the younger and stronger men.

Suddenly, Otter reined his pony to a stop. Jeremy pulled his horse alongside Otter's side and pulled up. Otter scowled and pointed to the tracks in the soil.

Jeremy's heart stopped. Two columns of horsemen had passed here less than an hour before. With two perfect columns of hoof prints, the horsemen had come from the north. The colonel had intercepted the trail and were now closing in on the slow-moving tribe.

The colonel was clever. He had led his cavalry troops cross country to a point north of where he expected the Crow to be, then rode along the river. He knew that this maneuver would eventually intercept the trail of a moving camp.

The cavalry was ahead of them now, between them and the unsuspecting Crow tribe as it retreated into the upper Big Horn Mountains. If the cavalry caught them before they reached the rugged higher elevations, they would be slaughtered on the open plain. The lances and arrows of the Crow were no match for the long rifles of the military opponent. The soldiers could stay out of range of the arrows and calmly decimate the tribe.

They all sensed the new urgency and quickly fell into place behind Otter. They pushed their horses into a long easy lope designed to cover the miles quickly. They must reach the tribe first and warn them of the rear attack.

Jeremy thought about Jennie. He had to reach the Crow before the cavalry. It would be her only chance. He choked down a sob and pushed the thought quickly from his mind.

They galloped only a few moments when Jeremy heard a shrill cry behind them.

Jeremy swung around on his bareback horse and saw a dozen Indians charging down the hillside. They were brandishing long feathered and painted lances. Their bows were ready and their quivers were full of arrows. Every horse and man was painted in bright reds and yellows. They were dressed for war.

Jeremy jammed his boots hard into his horse's flanks. The horse responded and opened up into a long easy stride that ate up the grassy hills. Otter rode fast and easily ahead of him while Medicine Elk strained to stay close to the other two. To fall behind now was instant death.

For the first minute, Jeremy did not understand. Who were they? They couldn't be Crow.

After several minutes of hard riding, Jeremy reached

down to pat the muscular heaving shoulder of his sweating horse. He suddenly realized that these pursuers would be Blackfoot. They must be part of the band that had attacked his own family and then been attacked at night by the Crow raiding party. They wanted revenge on the Crow.

Jeremy knew, too, that taking a white scalp would only heighten their pleasure.

Jeremy spurred his pony harder and leaned low across his back. They were unarmed and vulnerable. Speed was their only hope. He closed his eyes and said a quick prayer to his own God, then one to the god that protected the Crow.

They rode on and on over the grassy hills, desperately trying to stay ahead of the Blackfoot warriors who dogged them.

The Blackfoot closed in on them once. They let fly a half-dozen arrows that whistled past them. None of the arrows found anything but earth, however, and the chase continued on through the foothills.

Jeremy watched the cumulus clouds building up behind him, praying that it wouldn't rain. If it rained now, the ground would become muddy and slow them down. The horses would tire quickly and the chase would come to a final and disastrous end.

If they could hold out until dark, the pursuers might give up. Then the trio could disappear into the hills until tomorrow.

Suddenly, Medicine Elk started to catch up to him and Otter. Medicine Elk was driving his horse hard now, and slowly passed Jeremy.

He came alongside Otter and yelled a few words at him. Jeremy watched closely as they spoke and Otter looked to the northeast. There was a small cloud of dust rising lazily in the evening light. Medicine Elk spoke again, and Otter shook his head. Whatever Medicine Elk said, Otter said no.

Medicine Elk yelled again at Otter and split away from them, heading toward the dust cloud. Otter bellowed after him, then begrudgingly turned after him.

Jeremy had no choice but to follow the Indians, now

chasing each other in disagreement.

Jeremy glanced behind him. The Blackfoot were riding easily, pacing their mounts and leaning low over the manes of their horses. Each horse and man moved together as a single entity, dancing in perfect harmony in an effortless stride. Jeremy wondered how long he could keep his exhausted horse from stumbling, running at this breakneck speed.

Medicine Elk led Otter and Jeremy up a long low hill at an angle, until Medicine Elk topped the ridge. Jeremy watched in horror as the old man stopped, reared his horse and gave a blood-curdling war cry.

The shriek echoed in Jeremy's head. He knew that this would be Medicine Elk's last stand, his final encounter with the enemy.

Otter rode up alongside Medicine Elk's horse and grabbed the pony's halter. With all his weight, he jerked the horse back onto all four feet.

He, too, gave a wild war cry. Then they stabbed their horses' flanks with their moccasinned feet. The horses were off again, tearing along the ridge swiftly and in full view of the Blackfoot. Jeremy pushed his horse onward, trying to catch up to the two wild men.

He watched these two unarmed Indians ride at the top of the ridge. He didn't understand. By riding on the ridgeline, they would be seen on the skyline by anyone in the opposite valley, too. Whoever was creating the dust cloud on the other side of the ridge would easily spot them. If it was another band of Blackfoot, they would be pinched between them. It was suicide.

Jeremy finally gained the ridge in pursuit of his companions. As he reached the top, he quickly looked over his shoulder.

In the opposite valley were the bluecoated cavalry troops. That was worse. They had the Blackfoot in the valley on one side of them and the colonel in the valley on the other side. They were trapped.

The soldiers spurred their horses into a full run. They were less than three hundred yards down the slope. Jeremy turned his horse quickly and followed the ridge line. The Blackfoot and the cavalry raced after the three horsemen on the hogsback ridge, neither group realizing they were pursuing the same prey.

The ridge sloped off into an open meadow where the two gullies met. Jeremy glanced over his shoulder and realized they were all on a collision course. When they reached the bottom of the ridge line and entered the meadow, the Blackfoot would run squarely into the bluecoats.

Now Jeremy realized Medicine Elk's plan, and spurred his own horse harder and harder. The old man was pitting his enemies against each other, hoping to survive his own dangerous plan.

They had almost reached the meadow when the cavalry opened fire with their pistols. It was impossible to take aim while riding the horse at this pace, but Jeremy felt the lead balls whistle past him. He heard them slam harmlessly in the dirt next to his feet.

If the Blackfoot heard the rifles, the plan was lost. Jeremy hoped that the popping sounds of the rifles would be lost in the thunder of the hoofs. If the Blackfoot heard the gunfire, they would retreat, leaving the cavalry to overtake the three tired horsemen.

They dropped into the belly-deep grass of the meadow. The long low swale stretched out before them, meandering down into the larger river valley. Jeremy quickly looked behind him as the Blackfoot spurred their horses harder. Jeremy stayed low on his horse. He clung to the horse's mane with a knuckle-whitening grip.

Suddenly, a wild cry went up from the Blackfoot. They had ridden at breakneck speed into the meadow. Less than fifty yards away, the bluecoats thundered into the meadow from the adjoining draw.

The Blackfoot braves whooped savagely.

The colonel yelled and the troopers jerked their horses to a confused stop. Two horses reared, throwing their riders into the deep grass. Some of the soldiers fired wildly at the

Blackfoot, while others dropped into the tall grass.

The Blackfoot braves swung down from the backs of their speeding ponies, clinging to the lances and bows. They rolled in the tall grass and took up positions in the grass and sagebrush. Instantly, arrows rained into the ranks of the bluecoats and men began to crumple.

"Dismount. Take cover," came the cry from the startled colonel.

"Fire at will," a lieutenant yelled at the men.

The first shots came slowly, but soon increased. Two Blackfoot braves flipped backward off their horses.

Medicine Elk, Otter and Jeremy didn't slow down. They were unarmed. They couldn't stop. They pressed their mounts through the meadow as the sounds of battle faded behind them.

Finally, Otter slowed the pace to a gallop, then to a walk. They were out of sight of the battle, but they could still hear the loud rumbling of the long rifles that broke the prairie silence.

Both sides were pinned down at close range. The cavalry quickly found that their rifles were no real advantage at such close range. They took too long to reload. The arrows were deadly accurate and much faster in the hands of the Blackfoot.

The three horsemen slowed finally and stopped in a stand of wild rosebushes. Jeremy slipped from his horse. His knees were jelly and his unsettled stomach gnawed at his insides. His legs crumpled under him and he lay quietly on the ground, watching the cumulonimbus clouds. There was low rumbling thunder from the clouds that raced by to the north.

Out of the corner of his eye, he watched Medicine Elk slip loosely from his horse. The old Indian sprawled clumsily in the grass.

Otter dismounted stiffly and tied his horse to a rosebush. He quietly walked to Medicine Elk and knelt alongside him. With sudden surprise, Otter jabbered wildly at the old man.

Jeremy sat up and looked at the pair. Otter cradled Medicine Elk's head into his lap and laid his hand on the aging Indian's chest. When Otter lifted his hand, Jeremy saw the blood staining Otter's palm.

Jeremy scrambled to Medicine Elk's side. Blood oozed from a gaping wound in his chest. A cavalry slug had caught him in the back and exited just below the rib cage. The heavy bleeding stained the old man's buckskin and quilled shirt with dark reddish brown splotches.

The old man mumbled, moving gently into a sing-song chant. In a few moments, the chanting stopped and Medicine Elk closed his eyes.

Otter laid the old man's head back into the grass and stood up. His leggings were covered with the old man's blood. He looked as though his heart had been torn from his soul.

Jeremy knelt down and touched the warrior's chest. The blood was warm to his hands.

It was so much like a dream. The riding, the chase, the battle, and now this. They had traveled together for days and become friends. In spite of the language barrier, they had come to respect each other. Now, his friend was dead.

Medicine Elk's eyes were closed against his brittle face. Jeremy reached down and moved a wisp of raven hair that flitted in front of Medicine Elk's eyes. Gently, Jeremy pushed the errant hair back into his braids.

Medicine Elk had died the death of a warrior, not the death of an old man in the snow. It was a death that would be recounted through the generations as a death of bravery that saved a Crow village. If Medicine Elk had died in the winter snows, no one would have remembered him for more than a week. With no living descendants, he would have been forgotten quickly. But he died a hero, a warrior. Now, the legend of Medicine Elk would be told around the council fires at night as the old men taught the young braves about loyalty and bravery.

Jeremy stood up and wiped the blood onto his blue cavalry trousers. A soldier's rifle had finally felled this Crow warrior. A lifetime of counting coup on the Sioux and Blackfoot could not do it. A life of danger, hunger and wild animals could not defeat him. Only the white man's bullet could cut through him, returning him to his mother, the earth.

Suddenly, Otter spoke to someone standing behind Jeremy. Jeremy whirled to see two young braves mounted on horseback a few feet away. They held their long lances at their hips and pointed them menacingly at Jeremy.

Otter spoke softly to them and they lowered their lances. Jeremy then recognized one of the braves from the village and sighed with relief. They were evidently scouts who had been sent from the moving camp to investigate the gunfire. They were surprised to find their own people involved in the fray.

Otter and the two braves spoke in hushed tones for a few moments. One of the braves pointed to the southeast and continued to speak. Otter nodded.

Jeremy, Otter and the two braves boosted Medicine Elk's body onto his exhausted horse, laying him across its back. Jeremy and Otter mounted their own horses and moved off to the southeast, leading Medicine Elk's pinto.

The two braves cautiously turned toward the battleground to watch the fight from a safe position. The battle was close to the evening campsite and therefore dangerous to the tribe. The scouts would stay until the battle was finished.

They picked up the travois tracks again, and followed them for less than two miles. It was getting dark when Jeremy and Otter rode slowly into camp.

Their homecoming was less than joyous. There was so much activity in the camp that their intrusion was not even noticed until they were near the center of the camp.

A squaw screamed. Jeremy realized that he was still wearing the cavalry trousers and jacket. For a moment, the woman thought they were being attacked.

But Jeremy did not move toward her. His exhausted, beaten body slumped on his horse as he led Medicine Elk's horse. Another squaw grabbed the screamer and they scrambled to safety. Their arrival had been announced.

Otter rode up to a small buffalo-hide lean-to that was lashed between two cottonwoods. He dismounted and walked stiffly to the lean-to.

A pair of older warriors came out of the lean-to. Jeremy

recognized Braids His Hair On Top and the other one from his evening around the fire. As they approached Otter, they exchanged greetings.

Then one of the older braves pointed to Medicine Elk's body draped across the pinto.

Otter spoke slowly at first, then built up to a crescendo describing the battle, complete with hand gestures and simulations of the rifle fire. He pointed to Jeremy many times. Although Jeremy did not understand the Crow words, he knew all the time where Otter was as he told the story.

Finally, Jeremy slipped off his horse and approached Otter and the older braves. He stood shakily alongside Otter, teetering on the verge of exhaustion and collapse. He had trouble fixing his eyes on the three Indians.

Otter spoke again and patted his stomach. Braids His Hair On Top signaled to a squaw inside the lean-to, and within a few moments, Otter and Jeremy were seated in the lean-to devouring bowls of hot meat stew.

Jeremy could feel the strength injected into his veins as darkness fell on the camp. The warm greasy soup was a welcome feast to his troubled stomach. A hot meal was refreshing after days of chewing cold buffalo jerky and gritty pemmican. The last hot meal he had eaten was breakfast in the fort.

How many days ago was that? he wondered.

From outside the doorway of the makeshift tent came a greeting. Jeremy looked up and there stood Crazy Bear, the only Crow in the tribe who spoke English. Jeremy jumped to his feet.

"Crazy Bear," he said excitedly, "Where is my sister? Is she all right? I gotta see her."

Crazy Bear smiled and reached out to pat Jeremy's shoulders.

"You see her. You stay here. I get her."

Crazy Bear turned and disappeared into the twilight. In a few moments, he returned with Jennie. She was dressed in soft doeskin, a fabric much stronger and more practical than her old cotton dress. Her hair was greased and tied back into a single long braid. Her doeskin was decorated simply with porcupine quills and colored beads. A necklace of elk teeth hung above her young breasts.

Jeremy hesitated at first. She looked so natural in her Indian clothes. He closed his eyes and hugged her firmly.

"Are you okay?" he asked at last.

She sobbed, clinging tightly to him.

"Jennie, it's all right. I'm here now. You're safe. We can leave tomorrow. We'll go back to Missouri or on to Oregon. We'll go wherever you want."

Jennie loosed her hold on Jeremy slightly.

"You mean it?"

"Yes, I do. Are you okay?" he asked again.

She nodded simply and choked back her sobs. "Yeah, I'm okay. They fed me well and I have new clothes. Oh, Jeremy, I missed you so much. I was sure I'd never see you again."

"I was scared too, Jennie. But it's over now. We'll leave tomorrow."

Crazy Bear stood silently by them. He bowed his head, then spoke softly, "You cannot take her with you when you leave."

Jeremy's nostrils flared in anger.

"What do you mean, she can't come with me? She's my sister and I am taking her back!"

Crazy Bear hung his head and sighed.

"She is wife to a Crow warrior now. She was given to warrior because he was brave in battle with the Blackfoot. He captured her. He took two scalps. The chief said that the girl is now his wife."

"No!" Jeremy countered. "She leaves with me tomorrow."

Crazy Bear straightened up and regained his authoritative posture.

"You leave tomorrow if you want. The girl stays."

With that, he disappeared into the shadows.

Jeremy and Jennie moved away from the lean-to, but Crow guards stood nearby with lances to insure the young couple did not escape. A small fire sparked at their feet, throwing dancing shadows around them and the lean-to. The flickering light showed a tear forming in the corner of Jennie's eye.

"Is that true?" Jeremy asked her. "That part about being a wife to some warrior?"

Jennie nodded. "It is true. Crazy Bear told me the day you left that I would be this man's squaw. They were sure that you would never return. He told me that I belong to this man now and I must stay. But you have to take me with you when you leave. You can't leave me here with these people, Jeremy. You have to take me away!"

"Which Indian is it?"

Jennie shrugged. "I don't know his name. I've only seen him a few times. He stays away a lot. He's afraid of me, I think, because he won't talk to me. He has two other squaws that feed me and teach me the things that I have to do."

"Does this Indian...um...well...does he..."

Jennie squeezed his hand. "No. At night when I hear him move from his blanket, I pray that he doesn't come to mine. He never has. He goes to the blanket of one of his two squaws."

Jennie held his hand tight. Jeremy swallowed hard.

They were interrupted when Jeremy saw the two scouts return on horseback from the battle. The scouts headed for the lean-to and spoke to the Indians gathered there. Crazy Bear stepped from the shadows and listened to them. When they finished, Crazy Bear walked over to Jeremy and Jennie.

"Scouts say battle is over. Many white men killed. Many Blackfoot killed. Both go north, away from us."

Jeremy nodded. "Thanks."

Crazy Bear spoke to them, "I take her now. You see her tomorrow."

With that, they were gone. Jeremy stood quietly in the dying campfire light, shaking his head. He was confused. It didn't make any sense. He had fulfilled his mission. He had tried so hard, and now he found it was for nothing.

Crazy Bear returned soon.

"You sleep here," he said, pointing to the lean-to. "We

travel far tomorrow."
"When do I get to take my sister back?"
"Tomorrow we travel far. Now you sleep."
And he was gone again.

THIRTEEN

The camp was active all night. Jeremy listened to sounds that confused him as he tried to sleep.

The horses moved about nervously in their rope corral and a few men and women shuffled around in the firelight. He heard them as they repaired the leather and wood travois by the campfires, getting ready for tomorrow's journey.

But there was more tonight. He heard the chopping sounds on small trees and soft crashes as they fell in the grass. Somehow, Jeremy knew that it was not for firewood. There was plenty of deadfall all around them. It wasn't necessary to fell any trees here.

The women rustled in the grass and willow stands behind the camp. The pounding and scurrying continued until late into the night.

Otter shook Jeremy as the first rays of light illuminated the landscape. It was cold. He could see his warm breath condense into a white puffy cloud and diffuse into the morning mist.

Otter shook him again and spoke urgently to him.

Jeremy rose stiffly. The days of horseback riding and running had taken a toll on his body. His back ached and his buttocks were tight and sore. He struggled to his feet. He could hardly stand. The five or six hours of sleep that he did manage to steal did little to relieve his exhaustion. He was more than tired. He was weeks tired. It would take weeks to recover fully.

Otter led him quickly outside the night's campsite.

Jeremy stumbled along after him, cursing under his breath. Otter stopped, pointing to a nearby tree.

About eight feet above the ground in the first large crook of a lop-sided cottonwood tree was a small platform built with willow poles. It was laced with sticks and covered with grass. The platform, about six feet long and a foot and a half wide, sat precariously in the jagged angle in the cottonwood.

Jeremy gave Otter a curious look. Crazy Bear stepped up behind them. Jeremy watched silently as a dozen braves gathered around them. Each warrior was dressed in his finest feathers, quilled shirts and warpaint. Every Crow carried a decorated weapon, either a lance or bow. They stood unsmiling behind Crazy Bear.

From the far side of the camp, a small procession started toward them. Four brightly painted braves bore a litter made of willow poles and buffalo hides, carrying Medicine Elk's body.

They had dressed Medicine Elk in a fine feathered headdress, a buckskin shirt and leggings. His bloody buckskin shirt was gone and his face was washed clean. The new shirt was intricately beaded and the leggings bore long horsehair tassels with eagle feathers woven into the ends. Medicine Elk's face was painted for war with reds and yellows, the colors of the earth. At his side were a bow and four arrows, a small obsidian-bladed knife, and a ration of jerky and pemmican.

Behind the litter came the procession of braves, women

and children. Every man and boy carried a weapon, including knives, feathered lances and painted bows. Some of the women sobbed quietly as they moved to the cottonwood tree.

Crazy Bear turned toward Jeremy and nodded, "You."

"What?" Jeremy asked. "I don't understand."

"Medicine Elk dreamed you. He dreamed he would be lifted to the sky at sunrise by a young white man, not one of his own people. He told us of the dream in the winter before you came to our village. The sun rises now for him. You raise him to the bed of death. From there, he can start new life."

Jeremy swallowed hard. He remembered what Travis had told him about touching a dead Indian warrior or crossing the Indians' burial grounds. For a white man, it meant instant death.

Now, however, these Crow were asking him—no, telling him—to violate their own sacred custom.

Medicine Elk had been a friend. Jeremy had touched him when he was alive and felt his blood as he died. Now, though, he wasn't sure he could touch the dead body.

He knew about the dream, but he could not perform the ritual prescribed by the old man's dreams. He shook his head.

"I can't do it," he whispered.

Crazy Bear did not flinch. He turned to Braids His Hair On Top and addressed him strongly in Crow. The warrior turned to the people, raised his arms and began the eulogy. As he spoke, Crazy Bear translated quietly for Jeremy.

"Medicine Elk was a great warrior in his days. As a young man, he counted many coup on the Sioux, the Blackfoot, the Cheyenne. His lodgepole carried many scalps of his enemies.

"He took many wives and fathered many children. He taught his sons the importance of the tribe, the honor of battle, and the many ways of the mountains and plains.

"For the last three summers and winters, he did not fight or hunt. He was too old to hunt with the younger braves. There are not so many buffalo and they are harder to kill.

"He stayed with us and we fed him. The women sewed his clothes. We cared for him because he was wise and he told us many things that we should do.

"Medicine Elk was a dreamer, too. He dreamed many times about many things. He dreamed of things that we could not imagine. He dreamed of the future and how it would be for the Crow. At first, we called him a fool. But his dreams were always true. We learned to believe in his dreams.

"We did not understand his last dream. He dreamed that a young white man would arrive to take him to the mountain where he would die. We did not understand. It is our custom that the white man cannot touch the sacred burial beds. It is sacred to the Crow. It is our tradition that the strongest Crow warriors lift the old people into their last burial.

"Then the white man arrived, like Medicine Elk dreamed. Medicine Elk said that this was the young white man in his dream. The white man took him away to die.

"Medicine Elk left us as an old man who was worth nothing to the Crow anymore. He could not help us anymore. He could not hunt and his wisdom was not there. He left so that he could die.

"But Medicine Elk returned to us as a warrior yesterday. He tricked the Blackfoot and the bluecoats into killing each other. They fought each other instead of us. They killed each other instead of killing us.

"His courage saved us from a battle with the blue soldiers. We could not win that battle. We are traveling. There are too many women and children. Many of us would have died.

Braids His Hair On Top continued, "As reward for his bravery, the Great Spirit gave him a quick death, an honorable death. Medicine Elk's last day was not wasted.

"The young white man and Otter returned with Medicine Elk. They were chased by our enemies, the Blackfoot and the bluecoats. They showed their bravery on battlefield. They are living warriors. We honor them with our dead warrior, Medicine Elk.

"We sent Medicine Elk off as an old man. He came back to us a hero and Crow warrior. We raise his body to the sky on its first steps to a new life. We pray that he will find that new life that he dreamed."

There was a long silence among the people. They could not afford the luxury of a long memorial service, because they were to begin their day's travel at sunrise.

Crazy Bear finally broke the silence.

"You climb tree. We help lift body."

Jeremy nodded. He hadn't thought about this old man as a hero until now. Suddenly, he felt honored. The dreamer had chosen him to start him on his last journey.

Quickly, Jeremy scaled the trunk and straddled the crook.

A half-dozen braves lifted the corpse off the litter. They hoisted it high above their heads until Jeremy could first grab one arm, then both arms. He clutched the doeskin shirt at the chest and pulled the limp body into the tree alongside him. He wrestled the dead weight until it lay on the pole and grass platform.

Medicine Elk's eyes were closed now as if in sleep. Jeremy neatly arranged Medicine Elk's headdress and clothing. He laid the braids properly on the old man's chest and watched the feathers twitter softly in the morning breeze. He placed the ancient obsidian-bladed knife and food next to the body, sacredly, ceremoniously.

Jeremy looked up through the ragged cottonwood branches and felt the first morning breeze rustle the large shiny leaves. He was suddenly aware of the sun peeking over the low purple mountains to the east, spilling its life-giving brightness over the high northern plains.

It was sunrise. Within a few seconds, he had completed the task brought on him by the dream of an old Crow brave.

He felt lonely as he clung to the branches of the tree. Only the cold memories of this patriarch accompanied him now. He was separated by hundreds of years and thousands of miles from the silent crowd around the base of the tree. No one moved. No one spoke.

From his perch in the cottonwood tree, he could see the plains roll on forever to the north and south of him. To the west lay the jagged peaks and high alpine lakes, obstacles to settlers and frontiersmen. To the east sprouted the low rugged Pryors,

Big Horns and Little Wolf Mountains. These isolated ranges of pine-covered mountains offered protection and security to the Indians who fled the white man.

They were good mountains for the earthy people. There were high windy places where young braves could fast for days as they waited for their visions. If a warrior was pure, the visions would provide insights to their destinies.

There was water in countless small lakes and springs that rose up from the sandstone bluffs and granite cliffs. Game was plentiful and thousands of buffalo still thundered in the foothills. And as of yet, only a handful of white men had ever penetrated this isolated paradise.

Jeremy watched the landscape change before his eyes. He could see the land when white men like himself brought cattle and plows. In a few years, there wouldn't be room for the people of Medicine Elk. There wouldn't be room for Crow to hunt and fish. Their travels would be blocked by fences. Their culture would be buried.

His vision evolved, giving way to the sounds of a white man as he felled this very cottonwood tree. In his dream, he watched the man chop the tree, intent on burning it for firewood. The man, dressed in the dungarees of a Missouri farmer, would never know that this sacred tree had been the burial platform for a brave Crow warrior.

The breezes filled Jeremy's ears and rustled his hair. He was alone with Medicine Elk now. Alone in the world.

Suddenly, across the sky galloped a pale rider, jamming his moccasins hard into the flanks of a dappled pony. The rider held a lance above his head, its feathers flying in the gusting wind. Three other riders followed him on their ponies, heads high with their feathered headdresses flowing in the breeze. The first rider gave a single war cry and faded.

The vision was over.

Still entranced, Jeremy reached for Medicine Elk's stone-bladed knife. He pulled it slowly from the soft leather sheath and laid it in his palm. The handle was carved from an elk antler and fit his right hand easily. The stone-bladed knife was as old as the dead man. Like the old man, it was no longer useful now that the Crow could barter for steel trade-knives. The blade was rough and sharp in only a few places. Medicine Elk had not kept the obsidian blade chipped sharp.

Jeremy wasn't sure that it would be sharp enough.

He laid a clenched left fist on one of the cottonwood limbs, holding out only the index finger. With his right hand, he held the knife high as if it were an offering. He slowly brought it down to his index finger, laid it firmly on the first knuckle, took a deep breath, and pressed.

He heard the joint snap. The intense pain brought colors whirling in his eyes. He teetered as he straddled the limb. For a moment, he thought he would slip from the tree. He passed out, and instead, slumped against the main trunk.

When he opened his eyes a moment later, the joint was still there. The knuckle was broken by the stone blade, but hung loosely by a piece of stringy flesh. Blood formed rapidly on the end of the wound and dripped onto the platform.

Jeremy gripped the knife again and laid it on the finger. He pressed hard and jerked his left hand away. The severed joint rolled off the tree limb, down onto the platform and came to rest next to Medicine Elk's arm.

Jeremy could see the one rider again. He heard the war cry. He felt the wind blowing his hair. The knife slipped from his grip and he drifted into unconsciousness.

FOURTEEN

When Jeremy came to, he was lying on the ground in the lean-to. The sun was still low in the sky, just beginning to warm the earth for another day. Crazy Bear, Braids His Hair On Top and two squaws were kneeling around him.

His left hand throbbed mercilessly. He lifted it to see his wound. The women had wrapped the bleeding stub tightly in a piece of soft doeskin. As he moved it, he felt a greasy suave inside the wrapping.

As soon as he had opened his eyes, Braids His Hair On Top left. There was a big council, Crazy Bear told him. Jeremy drifted off again.

Shortly, Jeremy regained consciousness again. His knees were weak as he rose from the blanket.

Crazy Bear helped him as he stumbled out of the lean-to

and led him through the camp. The squaws and children had finished their packing to start another day of traveling. Horses skittered around, impatient with the delay. Dogs barked and small children raced back and forth in play.

Crazy Bear led Jeremy to a large circle of Indian men. They were no longer dressed in their ceremonial finery on this cool August morning. Now they wore greasy leather leggings and buckskin shirts with a few simple beaded patterns. Most had headbands of colored cloth or leather hide, and only a few sported feathers.

Braids His Hair On Top stood up as the two men approached. His hair hung loosely around his face, with one small braid on the right side that terminated in a worn eagle feather entwined in the hair. He was unpainted and his hair was ungreased.

Solemnly, he watched Jeremy try to stand.

Crazy Bear and Jeremy stopped in the center of the circle, an arm's length from Braids His Hair On Top. The murmuring stopped when Braids His Hair On Top raised his hand to speak. As he spoke, Crazy Bear translated.

"Young white man, you came to us to steal the girl that was ours. We understood why you wanted to steal her, but she belonged to us. We kill those that steal. But Medicine Elk dreamed about you and we did not kill you. When we sent you away with the old man, we did not plan to see you again, but you have found us and entered our hearts. You are a brave man."

Jeremy interrupted him, and spoke quickly, "I want my sister back now so that we can leave and go back to the white people."

When Crazy Bear translated the interruption, Braids His Hair On Top shook his head. He spoke again through the translator.

"The girl is a wife to one of my braves. She is his. He can do what he wants with her. You will leave us today. Three warriors will accompany you back to the fort of the white man."

"What if I want to stay here with my sister?"

Again, Crazy Bear translated for Braids His Hair On Top. "No. You have no choice. You leave."

Jeremy choked. He stiffly swallowed the lump that surfaced in his throat. After days and days of risking his life, fighting, running, and riding, he was exhausted.

The thought of Jennie had pulled him through the worst of it all. It had kept his head up and his body from failing him. It had given him direction and fortitude. He knew that he could win her release.

Now it all collapsed around him. Jennie was nowhere in sight. She was being kept away on purpose. Jeremy would be given a horse and taken to his own people.

His mind raced wildly. He would return in the night to steal her—if he could find the Crow again in these rugged mountains. He would stay until he could help her escape—but they would not let him. He would return with the cavalry—except they would throw him in jail the instant they saw him.

It seemed that he had no options. Jennie would stay here as a squaw to some Crow.

Braids His Hair On Top spoke again through Crazy Bear, "Before you leave, we want to honor you with gifts. You have been a brave warrior of the Crow and have saved the lives of many of my people. We will remember you as a friend."

Jeremy couldn't believe it! They were going to honor him as a friend and a warrior, yet they were keeping his sister as a prisoner and forcing him to leave the camp.

Two ponies were led into the circle by an Indian youth.

Braids His Hair On Top spoke through his translator, "These are my two best ponies from a large herd. They are fast and they will run forever. They will live as long as you."

With that, he handed Jeremy the rope halters of the two ponies.

The gift-giving continued around the circle. The Crow ceremoniously presented him with blankets for the horses, a blanket for himself, pemmican, a steel knife, a water pouch made from a buffalo bladder, fine eagle feathers, beaded moccasins, a shirt made of soft deerskin with elk teeth and porcupine quills embroidered on the front, a catlinite pipe wrapped in rabbitskin and other trinkets.

Each brave made a short speech with his gift, but Jeremy didn't hear Crazy Bear. His grief clouded the words.

"This is the last brave," Crazy Bear said as Otter stepped from beside Braids His Hair On Top.

Crazy Bear continued with the translations.

"I am Otter," the brave said, thumping his chest. He raised his arms high and spoke forcefully.

"I have counted many coup and stolen many horses from the Sioux and Blackfoot and Cheyenne. I am feared by them for I have cut many scalps from their people. Someday, I will be chief of this tribe, and I will have much power with my own people."

He dropped his hands to his side and looked Jeremy directly in the eyes.

"I am a great and strong warrior, and yet I am afraid of you. You have magic power. You are cunning like a fox. You go inside your enemy's camps and forts and leave without being wounded. You steal horses in the night and ride away from your enemies in the daylight.

"You do not complain when there is no food or water or blankets in the cold night. I am ashamed because I could not steal Medicine Elk from the white man's fort. But you, without a knife or rifle or a lance or a bow, take his arm and you walk out the big gate.

"When you put Medicine Elk on the platform, you cut off your finger. That is a Crow way, a way to remember him and honor him."

Otter stopped and looked at the circle of quiet young fighting men.

"None of his own people would do that because he was so old. You loved Medicine Elk more than his own people. I have one gift for you, Short Finger."

Otter turned and nodded to a woman who scurried off to the other side of the camp. While she was gone, Otter continued.

"I am giving you a squaw."

"I don't want a squaw," Jeremy quickly told Crazy Bear.

"Quiet. You will take gift," he snapped back.

"She is quiet," Otter went on, "and young and shy. She is like you. She will not complain of the long travel and bad food. She will work hard for you. You will take her when you leave and go back to the white people. I will go with you to a trading post on the big river where you will be safe."

The squaw returned, hurriedly pushing a young girl dressed in doeskin and moccasins. Her hair was greased and braided with feathers, beads and leather thongs. A necklace of mussel shells hung loosely about her neck. It was Jennie.

Suddenly, Jeremy realized that Otter was the brave that Jennie had told him about. Otter was the Indian who would not come to her blanket at night. He was the one who had taken scalps from the Blackfoot at the raid on their camp. It was this Crow who spoke no English and killed the mountain man, saving his life. It was this quiet man who had shared his camp for many days on a long and difficult journey.

"Short Finger, you are a brave man. I wish you were Crow. I hope that we never meet on the battlefield."

When Jennie saw Jeremy, she broke from the squaw's grip and leaped into his arms. Tears of joy filled her eyes. Jeremy hugged her tightly against his chest and stroked her greased hair.

"It's okay, sis. We can go now."